RIVERBEND FRIENDS™

Real, Not Perfect
Searching for Normal
The Me You See
Chasing the Spotlight

REAL, NOT PERFECT

Real, Not Perfect

RIVERBEND FRIENDS™

Stephanie Coleman

CREATED BY

Lissa Halls Johnson

A Focus on the Family Resource
Published by Tyndale House Publishers

27   26   25   24   23   22   21
7   6   5   4   3   2

Chapter

1

I TRIED NOT TO HEAR MY NAME being called, tried to just nudge my way through the humid pool room and out to freedom, but the call came again.

"Where's Tessa? Does anyone know where Tessa is?"

I had to get home, or I'd be late for the party. I couldn't be late for a party *I* was throwing. But if I didn't turn around—didn't do the right thing—I would spend the rest of the night with guilt simmering in my gut. Had my best friend, Mackenzie, been here to witness my moral crisis, she would've rolled her eyes and called me Good Girl Tessa.

I gave the double exit doors of the aquatic center one last longing look and then turned. "I'm here." I waved half-heartedly.

I hadn't recognized the voice, and I expected to see one of the senior boys or maybe a dad. I had *not* expected the new boy, Abraham.

His dark eyes locked with mine. "You're Tessa?"

My stomach squirmed. "Yep."

"Coach wants you."

Internally, I winced. I'd been here for several hours already. First with my own heats, and then helping wrangle the middle-school swimmers. I needed to get home, rush through my shower, and complete the last-minute tasks for Mackenzie's going-away party.

Externally, I put on a smile. "Okay, thanks."

I started back toward the blocks, where I could hear Coach Shauna yelling warm-up instructions to the young swimmers who were about to start their heats.

"I guess there's girl drama," Abraham half yelled as I shouldered my way through the crowd of exiting and entering families. I hadn't expected him to follow me. "And Coach Shauna was like 'Where's Tessa? We need Tessa.' I tried telling her that I'm qualified for girl drama, but she didn't buy it."

I laughed. "Should she have bought it?"

"I'm not *un*qualified. I have sisters."

I squeezed around a group of chattering pool moms and caught a glimpse of why I'd been summoned. Coach Shauna stood with Kayleigh, who at least had her swim cap on—a victory on its own—but was crying with her ropey eight-year-old arms crossed over her chest.

Good thing I hadn't just walked out the door.

I turned to Abraham and nearly bumped into him. For weeks, the other girls on swim team had been giggling about how cute Abraham Mitra was. He had dusky skin, long, curly eyelashes, and beautiful swim form. He was too flirtatious for my taste, but up close like this his charisma was hard to ignore.

There was no time for being flustered, however. Not when Kayleigh needed me. "My mom has probably been waiting in the parking lot for me for fifteen minutes. I'm gonna go tell her that I can't leave yet. Can you tell Coach and Kayleigh I'll be back in one minute?"

"No problem."

I elbowed through the thickening crowd. These all-ages practice meets were always chaos. For seasoned swimmers like me, this was a chance to practice before the upcoming season and to collect a few community service hours by helping with the younger swimmers. But for parents of new swimmers, even these practice meets appeared to be a cause for premature gray hair and bitten-off nails.

I pushed open the doors and breathed deeply. Even though it was August, the outdoor air felt comparatively cool, and the smell of not-chlorine was welcome.

"Hey, I was just about to come looking for you."

I startled at the sound of Alex's voice. "What are you doing here?"

He stood from a metal bench, surprising me all over again by how tall he'd gotten in the last year. For most of our friendship, I'd had the height advantage. "Your mom asked me to pick you up. Didn't she text you?"

That was weird. Mom had never asked Alex to pick me up before.

"Possibly, but I have no signal in there." I swung my swim bag around to dig through it for my phone. "Did she say why?"

"She's busy with party food, I guess."

"What about my dad?"

Alex replied with a shrug. "She didn't say."

"Sorry to interrogate you." I pulled out my phone and skimmed Mom's text. "Just says you'd be coming to pick me up. Huh."

Alex twirled his key fob around his finger. "She didn't make it sound like it was a big deal or anything was wrong."

I started to type a response to Mom, realized it didn't matter right now, and zipped my phone into its waterproof pocket. "Sorry to do this to you, especially when you've been sitting out here for who knows how long, but I can't go yet. You know Kayleigh from church whose Mom died a few months ago? I don't have time to explain it all now, but she needs me."

"Oh." Alex stopped twirling his fob. "Okay, no problem. I'll just hang out here."

"Alex, you really don't need to. I can walk home. It's not that far."

Alex frowned. "It's a couple of miles. And doesn't the party start at seven?"

"It does, but I take that shortcut trail through the forest—"

He shook his head, and his sandy hair flopped. "I don't want you going that way by yourself."

I rolled my eyes, even as I felt my cheeks heating, touched by his thoughtfulness. "It's well lit the whole way and full of moms and strollers. I'm fine. That's what I usually do, but it was supposed to rain, so Mom said she'd pick me up." I remembered Kayleigh's tear-streaked face and made myself stop explaining. "I have to get back in there. You can come in if you want, or you can go. I promise I can get home fine."

Alex reached past me, grabbed the door handle, and held it open. "I'll come in."

I tried to say, "Okay," in a casual and unaffected voice.

Mackenzie would have something to say about this situation, too. Since middle school, she'd been after me to "make it official" with Alex before other girls snapped him up. I hadn't disagreed . . . but I also hadn't known how I should go about "making it official" with a boy I used to invite to My Little Pony birthday parties. And then freshman year, when he met Leilani, my "snap him up" opportunity had expired.

I turned to Alex and found him wide-eyed, surveying the mess of parents, kids, and swim bags. "I know, it's Crazy Town. You can wait here. I'm gonna be over by the blocks, but I'll be done as soon as possible."

He pointed at my bag. "Want me to take that?"

"Uh, sure." With a quick smile, I swung it off my shoulder and handed it to him. "Thanks."

I rushed away, wondering if he was watching me, and trying to remember if I had brushed my hair after my heats. I was pretty sure I hadn't.

The pool deck wasn't quite as crowded now that most parents had either cleared out or found seats, and that made it easier to get back to Kayleigh. Coach Shauna was by the pool, organizing the kids into lanes for warm-ups. Kayleigh was turned to the wall now, and Abraham stood near her looking perplexed. When he spotted me approaching, his relief was clear.

I rested a hand on Kayleigh's trembling shoulder. "Hi, Kayleigh."

She sniffed but stayed facing the wall. "Hi." The word barely registered in the muggy room.

"I like your swim cap. It's new, right?"

"The old one pulled at my hair."

"I used to have one like that. The boys have it easy, huh?"

Beside me, Abraham snorted. "Not *that* easy."

Kayleigh glanced up at him but kept her arms wrapped around herself, then looked back at the wall. The room echoed with coaches yelling instructions, swimmers splashing into the water, and parents chatting in the stands. The noise was so familiar I hardly noticed it, but I wondered what Alex thought.

"Is your dad here?"

"Yeah."

Abraham murmured close to my ear, "He was already down here trying to convince her to get in the pool."

I nodded and asked, "Kayleigh, what stroke did Coach Shauna ask you to swim today?"

She wiped her nose with the back of her hand. "She said I could pick."

I figured. Early in the summer, right after Kayleigh's mom died, she would come to practice but refuse to get in the water. Her mom had always been the one to bring her, and even though Kayleigh didn't articulate it, our guess was that swimming without her mom in the bleachers just felt too painful. I knew Kayleigh's family a little bit from going to church together, and I had sat on the edge of the pool with her a number of times, hoping to get her back in the water—until her dad gave up and stopped bringing her.

Since this was Kayleigh's first time at the pool since June, I doubted Coach Shauna would be picky about what or how she swam. At this point, Coach would probably be fine no matter how I got her in the water and down the lane.

Then, my crazy thought bloomed into an actual idea. *Would Coach Shauna go for it? Would Kayleigh be willing to try?*

I turned to Abraham and whispered, "Do you want to stay here with Kayleigh, or do you want to ask Coach Shauna if I can swim warm-ups with her? We'll need a lane to ourselves."

Abraham glanced at Kayleigh's unyielding profile and headed for Coach Shauna. I watched him ask her, and then Coach gave me a thumbs-up and started moving swimmers out of the nearest lane.

I knelt beside Kayleigh. "What if I swam for you?"

She turned her face partly to me. Her blue eyes were bloodshot from crying. "What do you mean?"

"I mean, what if I did the swimming, and all you had to do was hold on to me?"

Kayleigh glanced at the pool, where the others on her team were butterflying up or down the lane. "How does that work?"

"Like a piggyback ride. Only since we'll be in the water, it will be more like a mermaid ride."

A smile flickered on her face. "But that's not allowed."

I pointed to the newly emptied lane. "Today it is."

I stripped down to my damp suit and offered my hand to Kayleigh. When she took it, I led her to the edge of the pool.

"I'm going to get in." I crouched close to make sure she heard. "And then you can get on my back."

I knew it was impossible to feel someone looking at you, but it seemed as though the whole room watched to see if today was the day Kayleigh would swim. I tried to push away the thought of Alex watching but found myself glancing at him anyway.

I bobbed a couple of times in the water, letting my body adjust to the cold, and then turned to Kayleigh. She looked down at me, her arms and legs both crossed.

"You don't have to swim," I told her. "All you have to do is hold on to me. I'll swim for you."

For a moment, I feared she would start crying all over again. But then she slowly lowered herself to the pool's edge, clasping her knees to her chest.

I held in my excitement, afraid it would freak her out. "There you go. Now let's just get your feet in the water."

After a few minutes of coaxing, I had her whole body in the water. Coach Shauna looked like she wanted to do cartwheels on the pool deck.

"Ready to go for a mermaid ride?" I asked.

Kayleigh hesitated, but then nodded. I took her arms, draped them around my shoulders, and then pushed off. We inched down the lane and had only reached the flags when I felt Kayleigh start kicking too.

"Mermaid rides are kinda slow," she said in my ear. Her voice sounded lighter, almost as if she was teasing me.

"Well, kick harder, then."

She did. In the lane beside us, kids her age blew by, swimming freestyle. I felt Kayleigh's head turn to look at them, her body slipping off mine just a bit.

"Carter always beats me at freestyle," she said as she watched him. In her voice, I could hear that bite of competitiveness that I always felt when in the water. "But not at breaststroke. He still can't get his feet right."

"You're fast at breaststroke," I said, even though I wasn't sure. "I bet if we raced to the wall, you could beat me."

Kayleigh hesitated a moment, and then slipped completely from my back. When she took off, delight surged in my heart. I trailed after her, doing breaststroke at half speed with chlorine burning my eyes and a huge smile on my face.

Kayleigh touched the wall, and every coach stopped what they were doing to cheer for her. A few of the parents joined in, and Kayleigh's dad was easy to spot now. He was the one standing, wiping his eyes, and applauding with the same gusto as parents of Olympic swimmers who just medaled.

Chapter
2

THE WIPERS ON ALEX'S HONDA CIVIC squeaked in protest every time they swiped the windshield. They were the soundtrack to our brief drive to our neighborhood, during which I filled him in on Kayleigh's backstory.

"I thought she was afraid of the water or something," he said.

"No, the girl's a fish. I think it's just that the memories of her mom are overwhelming at the pool."

At the traffic light, Alex glanced at me, his hazel eyes serious and soft all at once. "So, what you got Kayleigh to do at the pool . . . that was huge."

I felt myself blushing.

"And you did it."

"Kayleigh did it, really."

"But she wouldn't have if you hadn't helped her."

I shrugged and said, "Sometimes we need someone else to swim for us."

"I'm glad I got to be there for it." Alex smoothed his hair, a conversational habit of his for as long as I'd known him. "I've never seen you swim before. Like in a race, I mean."

I realized my ponytail was soaking Alex's passenger seat and pulled it over the front of my shoulder. "Uh, you know you *still* haven't seen me race. Today didn't count."

Alex grinned before saying, "Are you saying you let Kayleigh win?"

"Maybe."

"I'm not sure I believe you," he teased as he pulled up to my house. "I'll have to come to a swim meet this year and see."

"My first one is the same weekend as homecoming." I instantly regretted the words. Every time I said the word *homecoming*, the mortifying memory of last year surged to the surface. "You can park in the driveway."

"Clark needs the car, so I'm going to drop you off, pass the car off to him, and be back for party time." Alex shifted into park so the doors would unlock. "You doing okay? With Mackenzie moving, I mean."

My hand rested on the handle of the car door. There were too many ways to answer that question. I'd been trying to for the last month, when Mackenzie first told me she was moving to Palm Beach, Florida, where most of her mom's family lived. She was my best friend, so of course I didn't want her to move. But I also couldn't ignore that, a year ago, this news would've devastated me, and now—after freshman year left our friendship hanging by a thread—it felt less like I was losing something precious and more like I was losing the potential of something great. We'd been slowly mending what had come apart last year, and with her moving a thousand miles away, that would now be more complicated.

But that was too much to unload on Alex right now.

"I'm okay, thanks." I pulled the handle and popped open the door. "And thanks again for the ride. I really appreciate it."

"I was happy to." Alex seemed to hesitate. His smile was soft, almost shy. "I mean that."

Once upon a time, a smile like that would've made me think Alex was flirting. Trying to communicate something subtle to me. Now I knew better. "See you soon," I said, and shut the car door.

As I jogged through the mist to my front door, I mentally ticked through all that needed to happen. April and Leilani should be arriving in fifteen minutes with balloons and streamers. I could be showered by then, and maybe even get my hair blown dry before they arrived. Depending on if Mom needed help with food.

Tonight's party was really just a gathering of our friend group from middle school, plus Leilani. In addition to Mackenzie, the guest list was April, Leilani, Alex, and Michael. Cody was out of town, or our boy-girl ratio would've been even. We hadn't all gotten together for a while, and I felt weirdly nervous about a night that was supposed to be nothing more than hanging out with friends.

My house smelled of browned butter, and Ella Fitzgerald crooned on the speaker system—Mom's favorite cooking music. I kicked off my flip-flops and headed to the kitchen. I expected to find Mom humming to herself as she baked, but instead found Dad mixing seasoning into ground beef for sliders.

"Hey, kiddo. You just getting home?"

"Yeah. Where's Mom?"

"Dunno." Dad nodded toward the stand mixer, which contained some kind of batter. The counter space beside it was cluttered with measuring cups, a lemon, and containers of flour and sugar. A recipe book leaned against the backsplash. "Looks like she left mid-recipe. Grocery store, maybe?"

"She didn't tell you before she left?"

"I just got home a few minutes ago and found the place like this." Dad unscrewed the lid of the Worcestershire sauce. "Aren't your friends supposed to be here soon?"

"Yeah, I'm heading up to shower."

As I grabbed my belongings and jogged upstairs, the music turned from Ella to Jimi Hendrix. The Venn diagram of my parents' music taste hardly overlapped, so the battle for the stereo often resulted in the music just being turned off altogether. This was also true for movies, hobbies, and many other things. The list of what they agreed on was very short. Jesus, good food, and me, basically.

In my room, I noticed Mom had sent me a text message.

> **Out of cream and running to store. Should be back before party.**

She should be back anytime, then.

When I came downstairs fifteen minutes later, the music was off, and April and Leilani were tying balloons in various places around my living room. I'd pulled on a pair of jean shorts and a bright pink tank, but both April and Leilani were in cute summer dresses. I instantly felt underdressed for my own party.

"Wouldn't you know, there's a helium shortage," Leilani greeted me as she finished tying a bow. "We were limited to eight balloons. April even flirted with the cashier. Didn't work."

April's face scrunched like she'd smelled something bad. "I did. And he was gross."

"He wasn't gross." Leilani noticed something about the balloon tied to the mantel that she didn't like and crossed the room, her long, black ponytail swinging. "I'd rank him a five."

"Ew, no!" April shook her head at me. She wore glittery eyeshadow as if tonight was something besides dinner and hanging out with a few friends. "He was a three at best."

I glanced at my phone. "How about we stop ranking the poor party store employee and finish up? Mackenzie will be here anytime now."

"Tessa!" Mom called from the kitchen. Her cheerful voice had a noticeable strain to it, the kind that said, *I'm stressed, and I want you to know it, but I don't want our guests to know.* "Would you come here, please?"

"Coming." I cut through the living room to the kitchen, where Mom's artistic creativity sprawled across the counters in culinary form. Plates of fruit kebabs. Three kinds of cookies. A platter full of artfully arranged slider toppings. "Wow, it looks gr—"

"Can you go ask your father how much longer until the sliders are done?" Mom had her hands in soapy water and scrubbed a pot as though punishing it for bad behavior.

"Uh, sure."

The arch of her shoulders and pinch of her mouth made me think it had been a rough afternoon around here. I glanced again at the array of food. Mom had never before minded making treats for little gatherings like this. Often she created reasons to throw small parties just so she had an excuse to play with food.

"Are you okay?"

She didn't look at me or cease her scrubbing. "I'm fine. Just go ask your dad, okay?"

I hesitated only a moment longer and then headed for the back door. The rain had stopped and through the glass I saw that Dad stood beside the Weber kettle grill, a metal spatula in one hand and a Coke in the other as he chatted with Alex and Michael. Well, with Alex. Michael's head was ducked over his phone. Probably scrolling Twitter.

"Hey, princess," Dad said jovially as I opened the door.

The use of my dad's pet name for me was a little embarrassing. I avoided looking at Alex. "Mom wants to know how long until the sliders are done."

Dad checked the timer on his phone. "Tell her five more minutes."

"Okay. Mackenzie should be here soon."

"Roger that." Dad gestured to Alex and Michael with his

spatula. "I was just telling the boys here about your big birthday trip to Iceland."

I beamed at Dad, then at Alex. Michael still wasn't looking at me. "Just three months from yesterday." I bounced on my toes a couple of times. "I can*not* wait!"

Alex smiled and sipped his Coke for a moment before saying, "I told your dad that I would want to go in the summer because that whole twenty-four hours of daylight thing blows my mind, but your dad pointed out you can't see the northern lights that time of year. Which is kind of your goal."

"Why am I not surprised that you want to go in the summer?" Since second grade, Alex was That Kid who wore shorts whenever the temperature cracked thirty-two.

"I said you should go to a Sigur Rós concert," Michael said without looking up from his phone.

"I've never heard of them."

Now he looked up and winked at me. "That's how you know they're good."

Alex rolled his eyes. "I already told him weird Icelandic music might not be your thing." He gestured to my dad. "Or yours, Mr. Hart."

Dad grinned and raised the lid of the grill. "I don't know," he said. "When in Rome, as they say."

My phone buzzed. I expected it to be Mackenzie or maybe some random Instagram notification, but it was Mom's smiling picture that lit up my screen. *Wasn't she just on the other side of the door? Why was she calling me?*

I turned and looked through the window. She wasn't there.

"*Hasta luego*, princess," Michael said with a smirk as I opened the back door.

I ignored his taunting and answered my phone. "Mom?"

"How long until the sliders come off the grill?" Her voice had an unmistakably sharp edge.

That's what she was calling about? "Where are you?"

"The garage, getting the chocolate-covered strawberries out of the spare fridge. How long?"

"Dad said five minutes."

The door to the garage opened and I could hear in real time and in the slight echo on the phone as Mom said, "Five minutes since you went out there or five minutes from now?"

This was ridiculous. I hung up. "From when I went out there."

"Of course," Mom muttered as she dropped the strawberries onto the granite countertop with a clatter. "I *told* him to give me a five-minute warning."

This was so unlike her. She was prone to moods, but usually hosting a party put her in a great mood. *Was it the last-minute trip to the grocery store? Or that I'd come home later than I'd said?* "Can I help somehow?"

There was a knock on the front door and a simultaneous "Hello!" as Mackenzie let herself in.

"No." Mom looked me in the eyes for the first time since I came home. She wasn't wearing mascara or her signature black eyeliner, and it made her look tired. "I'm fine. Please just enjoy this last night with your friend."

Behind me, April and Leilani were greeting Mackenzie with such energy, you'd think it had been weeks since they'd seen each other. I held Mom's gaze a moment longer, but then she dropped eye contact and set about arranging glossy dipped strawberries onto a green platter.

Probably nothing, I told myself as I spun to face my friends. *She'll snap out of it before the party is even over.*

—⁂—

Despite the obstacle course of balloons in the living room, Mackenzie piled her plate with food and carried it out to the screened-in deck. Mom turned on the round twinkle lights even though it wasn't dark yet, and with the overhead fan going, the air was only mildly sticky.

Mackenzie placed herself in the wicker rocking chair and declared that she was the queen of the party. She talked even more than normal, made a joke of everything, and didn't seem to mind embarrassing others in the process. I'd known her since fifth grade, and I probably should've expected this buoyant mood. I'd seen many small versions of this act over the years, and extreme variations like this when her parents got divorced in seventh grade, and again last year when Noah, the upperclassman she'd been seeing most of freshman year, dumped her a week before prom. When Mackenzie felt low privately, her spirits seemed to soar publicly.

"Where's Cody?" Mackenzie asked as she poked Alex with a bare toe. "I was planning to throw myself at him tonight."

"Maybe that's why he's not here," Alex said without missing a beat.

Mackenzie stuck out her tongue. "Seriously, where is he?"

"Visiting family in Texas."

Mackenzie gave a dramatic groan. "Guess I missed my chance with him. I always kinda thought he looked like Captain America. Michael, no. Skip that song."

"But—"

"No. I'll have nothing in Spanish at my party. I can't sing along. Queen's orders."

Michael rolled his eyes but skipped the track.

"We should've tied the balloons out here," Leilani mused as she glanced around the porch. "April tried very hard to get you sixteen balloons."

As April and Leilani recounted the story for Mackenzie, I glanced at Alex. He raised his eyebrows at me. "She's really something tonight," he said in a low voice.

I glanced at Mackenzie, who laughed with too much gusto as April and Leilani again argued over the rank of party-store guy. "She's sad."

I wished it was just the two of us—Mackenzie and me—having a sleepover like we did when we were younger. Not that I didn't like having the others here, but I liked who Mackenzie was best when it was just the two of us. Ever since she'd dated Noah and hung out with his friends, she'd been a little different. She hadn't so much felt older and cooler to me, but rather like she wanted to be seen that way. Like a young girl at the grocery store dressed as Cinderella.

The hilarity of the party store employee expired, and Mackenzie sighed as she leaned back into the cushion. "Tessa, you have the perfect life."

Uh-oh. The mood pendulum was swinging the other way. "I dunno, you're the one who's about to be living on the beach."

"Yeah, but I have to be the new kid at school again. I hate that."

I'd lived in Riverbend, Indiana, all my life, so I had no life experience to offer.

Leilani rested a hand on Mackenzie's arm. "I get that, but you'll be fine. This time last year I was terrified about starting at Northside High, but you all were so welcoming to me. Palm Beach will feel like home in no time, I bet."

I tried not to visibly squirm. Leilani had moved here from Honolulu last year, and I hadn't always been "so welcoming." Alex had been smitten with her from day one, and even now, after watching her and Alex go through multiple breakups and hearing Alex swear he was over her, I had a hard time not mentally flagging her as a threat.

Mom pushed open the back door and called, "Don't forget about dessert in here, you guys!"

"Thanks, Mrs. Hart!" Mackenzie called. When the door shut, Mackenzie sighed as she sagged into the chair once more. "I'm going to miss your little parties, Tessa. Remember that sleepover when your mom made us doughnuts? Like for real, made us doughnuts. Or when your dad took us to Indy to see Taylor Swift? Your parents are the best."

"Chica's going to Iceland," Michael said without looking up from his phone. "You know that?"

"Yeah, I know," Mackenzie said glumly. "Tessa gets the dad who takes her to Iceland for her sixteenth, and I get a dad who invests his money in having the best gaming system. Like he's still a teenage boy."

"Hey," Alex protested teasingly.

"No offense intended to the teenage boys who are present. When you're in your forties and act like you're fourteen, it's not as charming."

I stood and gathered dirty plates. "Chocolate will cheer you up. I'll bring out dessert."

"So would better music." Mackenzie threw a balled-up napkin at Michael. "You have any lady singers on that iPhone of yours?"

Inside, the air conditioner made goosebumps rise on my arms. As I picked up two plates of cookies, Alex came through the back door with the dirty plates I hadn't been able to carry. "Thought I'd help."

"Oh, thanks."

He set them on top of the stack I'd brought in. "You're doing a good thing for Mackenzie."

I shrugged and said, "She's my best friend."

"Yeah, but I know it's been different this last year."

I didn't want to think about that. How Mackenzie basically ignored us all whenever being with Noah and his friends was an option. How she'd known that I was reeling from Alex crushing on Leilani but offered me nothing more than "I told you that you should've snapped him up before high school." It had felt like I lost both Alex and Mackenzie within a few weeks of each other.

I stuffed down the foul memories of freshman year. No reason to dwell on that.

"We all make mistakes," I said with a shrug. "Can you grab those two cookie plates?"

Outside, Michael had cranked a song I only vaguely recognized, but Mackenzie and April knew it. They were in the middle of laughing as they botched a TikTok dance routine. Leilani had her legs tucked up under her on the wicker couch as she scrolled on her phone. She looked up at us and made a "They're being embarrassing," kind of face. Or, no. She was looking behind me and exchanging that expression with Alex.

As Alex offered her the plate of cookies, I curled into my own chair and distracted myself with Instagram. Abraham Mitra had requested to follow me. That was interesting. In his profile picture, he made a serious face at the camera, black hair coifed perfectly. Since I nearly always saw him grinning and hair slick with water, would I have even recognized him? Not surprisingly, three other girls on my swim team already followed him. I clicked Accept and followed back.

Alex loomed over me, cookie plate in hand. "Whatcha doing?"

I tucked my phone away. The word *nothing* was on the tip of my tongue, but just before it came out, my stomach churned with jealousy as I remembered him and Leilani. "A guy from my swim team requested to follow me on Instagram."

I took a chocolate chip cookie and tried to ignore the weird bite of guilt in my gut. But why should I feel guilty? What I said was 100 percent true. And Alex was just my friend. That had been made abundantly clear over and over freshman year. But I knew I'd said it hoping to make Alex jealous.

"Interesting." Alex's teasing lilt told me I'd failed. "Was it maybe that guy who was walking out with you after Kayleigh swam? Abe, or whatever?"

Abraham had been leaving at the same time as me, and Alex

was waiting there with my swim bag. It had seemed weird not to introduce them.

"Abraham, yeah." I broke my cookie in half.

"Can't say I'm too surprised." Alex lingered, as if waiting for me to reply.

I stuffed half my cookie in my mouth and offered a closed-mouth smile, to which he rolled his eyes and turned to set the cookies on the patio table.

Mackenzie's energy level steadily rose as the clock ticked closer to eleven, the time her mom said she needed her home. At 10:45, Mackenzie raised her cup of lemonade and said in a grave voice, "I think Tessa should give a speech."

I'd been feeling a little drowsy—my day of swimming and party prep catching up with me—but snapped awake as all eyes turned to me. "Wait, what?"

"A speech." Mackenzie blew her long, auburn bangs out of her face. "You know how in movies when someone is moving away or becomes homecoming queen, somebody gives a speech?"

"That never happens in real life, tho—"

"Who cares about real life? I've been your best friend since elementary school." Mackenzie swallowed hard and blinked rapidly. "I leave tomorrow. Who knows when you'll see me again? Now, give me a speech."

Leilani and Michael both returned to scrolling their phones. April giggled and followed Mackenzie's lead, as always. "Speech, speech, speech," she chanted in a soft voice.

I looked at Alex, as though he would save me, but he only chuckled and shrugged.

"Um, okay. Well, Mackenzie is my best friend—"

"Tessa! No. You have to stand. Nobody sits down and gives a speech."

I rolled my eyes. "Would you like to give the speech? You seem to have a very clear idea of how this should go."

"No, but I will give you an example." Mackenzie popped to her feet, held out her plastic cup, and smiled at each one of us before saying, "I've known Tessa since the fifth grade. While everybody else just tolerated the new kid, Tessa went out of her way to make sure I was included in things and had a place to sit."

Mackenzie paused as her chin trembled.

"That's overselling me," I said thickly as tears clouded my own eyes.

"Shh. No interrupting a speech." Mackenzie took another moment and then carried on, "I've always been welcome at her house, and sometimes it's felt more like my home than the house I live in. She's always taken care of me, even when I was stupid, and she never asks for anything in return. Let's all raise our cups to Tessa Hart."

"To Tessa," my friends echoed.

I averted my gaze into my cup of Dr Pepper and closed my eyes. My throat was cinched so tight I couldn't swallow.

"*That* is how you give a speech." Mackenzie said in a watery voice. "Now it's your turn."

"If you'd told me this was an important aspect of the party for you, I would've prepared something," I grumbled as I stood.

"I know you would've." Mackenzie grinned and said, "I don't want a perfect, prepared statement. I just want it to be real."

I rolled my eyes, smoothed my shorts, and then held up my cup in the manner she'd modeled. "Okay, fine. What can I say about Mackenzie?" And then, looking at her expectant face, bright in the glow of the twinkle lights, I knew. "So everybody knows Mackenzie likes to have a good time. Well, our final art project in sixth grade was making clay mugs. I'd been so excited about it and worked really hard on my mug."

I fanned my face as tears blurred my vision. "Finally, the cups were baked and finished and handed out. Ms. Phillips put lemonade in them for all of us, and Mackenzie says, 'Let's do cheers.' And she clinks her cup against mine, and my handle breaks off. The cup falls to the ground and breaks into dozens of pieces."

April handed me a Kleenex, and I wiped my eyes, probably smearing mascara into my hairline. "I was so mad. Of course, it was the end of the school year, so there was no time for me to make a new cup or anything. Mackenzie felt horrible and swore to me she would fix it. I blew it off because I was so angry with her."

"Though you told me a hundred times everything was fine," Mackenzie said as she wiped her own eyes. "Heaven forbid Good Girl Tessa feel something like anger."

"Quiet. No interrupting a toast." I fixed her with a mock stern look that made her giggle. "So, early the next morning, Mackenzie showed up at my house. She had spent hours gluing the whole cup back together. Every little shard was there. It couldn't hold liquid—we tried—but it still meant so much to me that she would do that. It works great for holding pens and pencils on my desk." I smiled at her, even though my chin trembled. I managed to say, "Mackenzie, even if you break things, you've proven yourself amazing at taking responsibility and fixing them. I'm going to miss you like crazy." I held up my cup and could barely say, "To Mackenzie."

"To Mackenzie!" the others chorused.

Mackenzie beamed at me. "Best speech ever."

Chapter
3

I awoke the next morning to bright sun streaming through the gaps in my curtains. *Had Mom and Dad decided not to wake me for church?* Dad helped in the tech booth most Sundays and was always gone early. I usually rode with Mom, because even on the Sundays when she served in children's ministry, she left later than Dad. I glanced at my phone—8:30. She might still be here.

I pushed back the covers, pulled on my Northside High sweatshirt, and clattered downstairs.

Mom and Dad sat in their respective chairs, both dressed, but neither in church clothes. Mom's face had a pinched expression to it, so whatever mood she'd been in last night hadn't yet worn off. When I entered, she turned away and faced the back windows.

"Good morning, Tessa," Dad greeted me in an even voice. He looked tired, but not cranky. "How'd the rest of the party go?"

"Really well, I think." I hovered in the doorway and stuffed my hands in my hoodie pocket. "Thanks for letting me have it."

"Anytime." Dad glanced at Mom, as if expecting her to chime in. She kept her face averted.

"Is something wrong?"

Dad brought his gaze back to mine. "Why don't you have a seat, Tessa."

So, yes. Something was wrong. My mind blurred with possibilities as I crossed the room. *Could Dad have lost his job? Were Grandma and Grandpa okay?*

I perched on the edge of the leather couch. "What is it?"

Dad sighed and rubbed at the back of his neck. "There's no easy way to tell you this, honey." He swallowed. Again, he glanced at Mom. She still did not return the look. So he took another deep breath. "Your mother and I are getting divorced."

I froze.

Dad's gaze held steady on me, and from this angle, I could see Mom's clenched jaw. The room was bright with the rising sun, and my underarms grew sticky as I struggled to understand what he'd just said.

"Divorced." The word emerged slowly, same as when I tested out new French vocabulary.

Dad nodded and nudged his glasses back into place. "I'm sure you've noticed that things have been tense around here these last few months," he said.

He seemed to be waiting for me to answer.

"No, I haven't, actually."

"Well, they have been. And it's become clear to your mother and me that it's unfair to carry on like this, and that divorcing is the best option."

I looked at Mom, who still had her face averted. There were too many questions swirling in my head, and I couldn't grasp hold of a single one. I tried to keep my words as measured and calm as Dad's as I said, "But this doesn't make sense."

Dad nodded, as if he agreed. Though obviously he didn't, since he was the one saying divorce was the best option. "It's normal to feel that way, Tessa."

He continued to look at me in that steady way of his. The sunlight glinted off his glasses, obscuring his eyes.

Was that all he was going to say? Was it now my turn to talk? My chest ached as if my swelling panic had claws.

"Okay . . . but . . ." I glanced at Mom again. Still she looked away, but her eyes were squeezed shut. "You guys are happy together."

They were, right? I tried to scroll my brain for the last time I'd seen them actually doing something just the two of them.

Dad nodded again, which made that dark thing in my chest thrash. He said, "I know it's difficult to understand, Tessa, but we want you to know that you're our number one priority in this. You're not going to have to move or change schools or anything like that. We're committed to making this as easy on you as possible."

"Um, okay."

I hadn't even started on the spiral of all the ways a divorce changed a life. A family. I felt like I had as a little kid when they tried to teach me to play spades. I was still staring at my hand, trying to figure out what these cards even meant, while Dad talked through strategy for if someone bid nil. I hadn't even known what he meant.

I pulled my knees up to my chest and felt tears slip down my cheeks. When I spoke again, my voice held a pitch of hysteria. "But I don't understand why this is happening."

"We know this will take some time to process, but you've probably noticed that in these last few months—"

"I haven't." My volume rose. "I said that already. To me, you guys have seemed totally fine. Was that an act?" I flicked my gaze between them, and anger roiled in my chest as Mom continued to stare out that stupid window. "Mom?"

Dad sat up straight in his chair. "Parents never want their kids to worry, so your mom and I were certainly trying to behave like everything was okay, but—"

"When Mackenzie's parents got divorced, you told me that would never happen to you guys. You told me divorce was wrong. That you would always work things out."

Dad frowned. "I don't remember that conversation specifically, but—"

"Mom said it." I didn't mean for my voice to get so loud, but I'd lost control over my volume. "That's what you told me, Mom. So what happened?"

Finally—*finally*—Mom turned to me. Her red, swollen eyes called back the memory of Kayleigh's face only yesterday afternoon. And more than that, the realization that I had noticed her looking haggard yesterday. I thought she was just irritable about having to go to the grocery store.

"I meant every word of that, Tessa." Mom's voice sounded as though she'd rubbed it with sandpaper. "I still do. This divorce is not what *I* want."

I looked to Dad, expecting a disagreement. Instead, he looked down at his hands, which were folded on his lap. He wore no wedding band, and after a summer of yardwork and running outdoors, the newly exposed ring of skin was pale.

"Dad?" The word came out strangled.

Dad stayed silent.

"Would you like to tell her what's been going on, David?" Mom's invitation had steel woven through it. "Or would you like for me to?"

The only sound in the room was the antique clock on the mantel, ticking away the seconds of this agonizing conversation. Dad audibly exhaled for five long seconds before he looked me in the eye again. "Tessa, sometimes love is very complica—"

"No!" Mom snapped. She sat up in her chair. "Just be straight with her."

"I'm trying to." Dad cut her an angry look of his own, the first time in this conversation that he'd looked something besides calm and in control. "But you're interrupting me."

"Because you're trying to justify to our daughter what you've done instead of just telling her."

"I'm not trying to justify it. I'm not saying what I did was entirely right—"

"*Nothing* about what you did is right. *Nothing.*"

Dad blinked several times at her. "We can discuss that later, Carrie. Right now, I'd like to continue my conversation with Tessa."

Mom's eyes held fire as Dad turned back to me. Seeing him dismiss her in that way made the creature in my chest feel as though it had turned to ice.

"Tessa, as I was saying, at your age, love might seem very simple—"

"Your father has been having an affair since February," Mom said in a graveled voice.

Dad swore under his breath.

"Dad," I gasped as revulsion rippled through my body. "That can't be true."

My dad—my levelheaded, steadfast, churchgoing, bald father—returned to staring at his lap.

"That can't be true." The words came out as if I was begging. His form blurred as tears filled my eyes. "That's not true."

Dad's confirmation was there in the sad way he said my name. "Tessa . . ."

"No." My feet took steps backward without me even realizing I had stood. "How could you do something so disgusting?"

"It's very complicated—"

"No, it isn't. You're married to Mom. You're in love with Mom."

"While I'll always care about your mom—"

"Divorcing somebody isn't caring for them. *Cheating* on them isn't caring."

"It's just not that simple—"

"It really is." The words sounded as though I'd crafted them from that ice sitting in my chest. "And I'm not interested in listening to any more of your excuses."

I strode out of the room and thundered up the staircase. The double doors to their bedroom were open, like always, and the pile of zipped suitcases that I hadn't noticed on my way downstairs halted my steps.

I stepped into the room and looked around with a critical eye. The wedding portrait that normally hung over their four-poster bed was gone, though the evidence was there. Unlike the pale ring around my father's finger, the rectangle of paint that had been concealed under the portrait was a darker shade of gray.

I walked into the closet. Dad's corner of collared shirts in muted tones of gray and blue were all gone, as were his collection of khaki pants and running shoes.

How could this be happening with a man like my father?

He was a man who sought order and rhythm in all aspects of life. Who wanted a banana and a carton of Greek yogurt for breakfast every morning. Who ran faithfully every day. Who had been raised in the church, and then chose to raise me in the church as well. Who never gave me a safe sex talk, but rather a "no sex until you're married" talk.

How could that dad be the same dad who was packing his bags and telling me love was too complicated for me to understand right now?

The swelling of an argument in the living room carried up the staircase, and Mom's volume rose to the point where I could hear every word clearly.

"You don't get to tell me to act rationally! I pretended all day yesterday that everything was fine. I'll yell all I want now!"

Was I really so self-absorbed that I couldn't detect my parents' marriage imploding when we lived under the same roof?

I tiptoed to the top of the stairs. Dad responded with something, but all I could catch was the name Rebecca. *Was that the woman's name? Or a counselor they'd been seeing? Did I know the woman Dad had cheated with?*

"David, you know what you did is wrong, and one day you're going to wake up and realize that you threw away everything and can't get it back. And when that happens, Tessa and I will not be sitting around waiting for you."

"I know you're angry, but don't pretend Tessa doesn't need a father. We both know . . ."

I leaned against the banister, straining to hear, but I couldn't make out the rest of Dad's words.

"Don't you dare bring my father into this." Mom's words were low and venomous. "He was far from the perfect dad, but at least we always knew what he was. At least he didn't hide behind some Jesus-loving, family-man mask for years."

My phone vibrated in my hoodie pocket. I pulled it out and blinked at the text from Izzy, a friend from church.

> **Are you here? Want to come over and bake cupcakes after service?**

With my life crumbling around me, how was it possible the world kept turning for everybody else? How could it be that as my mom yelled, "You can have your stupid Rebecca and your stupid Facebook! Tessa and I don't need you!" my friend Izzy was at church considering making a dessert just for fun.

I swiped away Izzy's question and opened my chat thread with Mackenzie.

Can you talk? I just found out my parents—I had to wipe my eyes before I could finish the message—**are getting a divorce.**

Downstairs, Mom snapped, "There's nothing you can say to

convince me this is 'God's best' for us all. Why don't you just finish packing so you can go be where you actually want to be?"

I hustled to the end of the hall, slammed my bedroom door, and turned the lock. My whole body shook, even though I was sweaty. I collapsed into my beanbag chair and curled into a ball.

Dad came upstairs, his steps evenly spaced. Mom usually jogged up, so it was easy to tell, even from behind my closed door, who was coming. They approached most things in life differently, and often joked about being an odd couple—Mom the fiery artist and Dad the level-headed statistician.

"Opposites attract," Dad would say and squeeze her close to him. They would both smile and look at each other with adoration.

I doubled over as that dark creature in my chest roared. I pulled my hood as far over my face as I could. I just wanted this to all go away. I just wanted everything to be fine.

Dad's even footsteps came down the hall. He stood outside my door for a moment before knocking. "Tessa, honey?"

"What?" The syllable came out flat and not weepy, for which I felt grateful.

"May I come in?"

"No."

"I'm about to go. I'd . . . I'd like to give you a hug or something . . ."

"No."

Dad sighed loud enough for me to hear. He tried the doorknob, and fury swelled in my chest. Hadn't I said *no*?

"Tessa, I know you're angry. I get that. I would be, too, in your situation."

I stayed silent. *Did he think I was going to engage in a conversation through the door?*

"This is hard on me, too," Dad said as the seconds ticked away. "I know it's difficult to understand now, but it's the right thing to do."

How could you think that? How could you convince yourself that leaving your wife of nearly twenty years was ever the right thing to do? My teeth ground together as I tried to keep all the angry words locked inside, and pain radiated through my jaw.

"Tessa, honey, if you would please just open your door. I know this is hard, but if we could just talk for a few minutes before I go. We've always been the rational ones in this house."

How dare he group me with himself. How dare he belittle Mom, as if she was overreacting to what he'd done. As if this was some obvious fault or weakness of hers.

I spun toward my desk, snatched my ceramic pencil cup, and chucked it at the door with all my strength. The heavy clay cup—the one Mackenzie had painstakingly glued back together for me—gouged the door and fell to pieces while pens and pencils exploded across my bedroom.

"Tessa?" The doorknob jiggled. "Are you okay? What was that?"

"That meant go away." I wrapped the sweatshirt tighter around me, and because the cup had hurt only my door and not my dad, I added, "We don't need you here. Mom and I are fine without you."

I pulled my head inside the hoodie, like a turtle, to muffle my crying. Dad must not have stood outside my door too long, because minutes later, the garage door rose and then lowered with his departure.

Chapter

4

WHEN I FINALLY STUCK OUT MY HEAD, my bedroom was blindingly bright. I'd lived in this room my entire life, first with pink walls and a crib, then even pinker walls and a mermaid theme. Last October, Mom and Dad gifted me a room makeover for my fifteenth birthday, so now everything was a soft aqua color with driftwood-gray furniture. Even ten months later, I still sometimes felt surprised by the not-pink walls.

I sat up and caught sight of myself in my full-length mirror. My straight, brown hair hung limp and my long bangs jutted at an odd angle. My eyes were puffy like Mom's had been, and I couldn't see the crust of dried tears, but I felt it. I wiped at my clumpy eyelashes with the sleeves of my hoodie.

I hunted through my pocket for my phone. There was still no response from Mackenzie because I'd never actually sent the message. Izzy had sent another plea full of cupcake emojis and question marks. Busy today but thanks, I typed.

When I stood, my legs ached from being curled up for so long. Showering sounded tempting, but I needed to check on Mom, so instead I opted for a headband and finger-combing my hair into a quick knot.

A new message came from Izzy, a weeping emoji. *Tell me about it*, I thought, and swiped the message away.

I stepped on something cold and solid as I walked to the door. Part of the broken ceramic cup, and fortunately, it was a curved side. I stretched out my hoodie like an apron and gathered the broken pieces, as well as the spray of pencils, pens, and highlighters. I dumped the mess on my desk to deal with later. On my way out of my bedroom, I ran my finger over the gouged door. I could fill it with putty, sand it, paint it a matching white, and you'd never know it had happened. The door would look completely normal again.

How nice for it.

I unlocked and opened my door. The house was silent. No Ella Fitzgerald, Billie Holiday, or Frank Sinatra. Maybe Mom was in the basement, puttering with art supplies. When Mom was stressed, nothing in the house was safe from being rearranged, repainted, or recovered.

The suitcases, I couldn't help noting as I passed Mom and Dad's bedroom, were gone.

I clenched my jaw and crept down the stairs. Now I could hear the soft sounds of the television. I found Mom on the couch with a cable-knit throw wrapped around her and her gaze glued to the screen as though she was actually interested in the infomercial for those military-grade sunglasses.

She hadn't seen me yet, and I took the opportunity to really look at her, because apparently, I hadn't been doing a good job of that. Her hair had more silver than brown these days, and with the shadows under her puffy eyes and no smile to hold up the corners of her mouth, she looked older than her forty-four years.

What did the other woman look like?

I flushed with shame as soon as I wondered, because it shouldn't matter what she looked like. When you were married, you shouldn't have to compete with other women for your husband's affections.

My heart clenched like a fist in my chest. *We're going to be fine,* I told myself. That's what I told Dad before he left, and I would do whatever I could to make that be true. I would be fine. Mom would be fine. We didn't need him.

I straightened my shoulders and infused my voice with confidence. "Hey, Mom."

She startled. "Oh, Tessa." She placed a hand over her heart. "I didn't hear you."

On the coffee table was a pile of used Kleenex, but otherwise the living room looked exactly as it did an hour ago.

"How are you, kiddo?" she asked as I sunk onto the couch beside her.

"I don't know." I kept my eyes on the TV. "Not great."

Mom grasped my fingers. "I'm so sorry, Tessa."

I turned to look at her. Her eyes filled with tears, and she shook her head. As if there was more she'd been planning to say but now couldn't.

"Mom, this isn't your fault." I squeezed her hand.

"I practically yelled at you that your dad was having an affair." Her voice pitched higher with each word. "I didn't mean to do that."

"You didn't yell. You were very calm." I hugged her as best I could from this angle. "Even if you had yelled, it wouldn't have mattered. That news was going to land hard however you said it."

Mom began to shake against me. "How can this be happening?" she wept. "What are we going to do?"

I don't know.

Maybe Dad would change his mind? Maybe he wasn't actually moving in with someone else, like Mom had said. Maybe this was just some weird midlife crisis, and he'd realize his mistake and come home in a couple of weeks. Mom and Dad could get some counseling and life would go back to normal.

Mom stopped crying and looked at me in horror. "Honey. Your Iceland trip."

The words felt like a full-body slam. "Oh . . ." *How had I not thought of that yet? What would happen?*

"I'm sure you'll still go," Mom said in a rush.

All I could do was blink. An hour ago, my dad was my hero. I knew he loved me wholeheartedly and would be there for me no matter what. Now I felt as though I knew nothing for sure.

"Your dad will make sure the trip happens," Mom continued. "You two have been planning it for a year. He would never break that promise to you."

I thought of the ring of skin around his finger, pale from removing a ring he'd worn almost twenty years. "Wouldn't he," I said as a statement rather than a question.

Mom blurred before me as the reality of what had happened began to play out in the long term. *Even if Dad did change his mind in a few weeks, healing wouldn't be an easy fix, would it? How could we ever trust him again?*

I laid my head in Mom's lap and wept through an entire commercial break. Then I just laid there and let tears dry on my face as I watched kangaroos hopping in the desert on whatever nature show this was. Truth was, I'd never seen my mom watch a nature show.

"What do we do now?" I asked, my voice froggy and pitiful.

"I don't know, honey." Her fingers scratched softly across my back. "I guess one step at a time. Breakfast, maybe."

"I'm not hungry."

"Yeah." She sighed. "Me neither."

We watched another commercial break in silence. "How did you find out?"

"Your father told me yesterday." Mom's voice sounded hollow, as though she'd used up all her emotion in the last twenty-four hours.

Tears tickled my eyes. And then she'd had to throw a party. While pretending nothing was wrong. What a terrible day.

"I knew things weren't great between us," she continued. "I'd suggested counseling a couple of times, but he didn't want to go. I even tried suggesting it yesterday, because I'm just that stupid."

"It's not stupid to fight for your marriage."

"It was stupid of me not to realize he'd already made up his mind, but I just couldn't believe he'd fallen in love with somebody else." Mom muffled her sobs behind a tissue, and every tear she wiped away made my heart feel increasingly hard toward my dad. *How could he do this to her? To us?*

My words sounded like I'd made them of steel when I asked, "Do I know her?"

"I don't think so. Her name's Rebecca Simmons. They dated in high school. Reconnected on Facebook last summer when she moved back to town to teach kindergarten." She took a deep breath. Shrugged. "Started seeing each other sometime in February."

The thought of my dad secretly sending messages and sneaking around with an ex-girlfriend while at the same time sharing a roof with my mom made my stomach churn. If I'd eaten breakfast, I probably would've thrown it up.

"Have you met her?"

Mom's jaw tightened, and she shook her head. "I looked her up on Facebook, though. She teaches at Trailwood. We have about a dozen mutual friends, but that's Riverbend for you. I can't throw a stone without hitting someone your dad or your grandparents grew up with, fought with, worked with, whatever."

Oh, Grandma and Grandpa. What would they think about Dad? Did they know already? They would condemn what he'd done, I imagined, but he was still their son . . .

Mom's hand reached out and covered my own. I realized my eyes had grown teary.

"I can practically see your thoughts racing, Tessa. I know this is so, so much."

I nodded and made myself look at her. Her vulnerable, wounded expression now had worry sitting alongside it. Like Mom was an emotional Jenga game. I'd had much more practice dealing with her worry, at least. Mom was often worried that I was pushing myself too hard, being too hard on myself, not having enough fun, and so forth.

"We'll be fine." I squeezed her hand and willed the words to be true. "This is hard right now, but we're going to get through this together just fine."

That didn't feel true right now, not at all. But that's what I'd told Dad just before he'd left, and I was determined to be true to my word, even if he no longer valued the concept.

On the TV, a sea turtle swam in blue waters as a British man narrated her movements and offered facts about her habitat, age, and body. I studied her hard shell as she glided among the coral reefs, unperturbed by her surroundings. That would be me, I decided. Dad could come at me however he liked, and I would just swim away, protected by my hard exterior. And nobody—least of all Dad—would know how I ached within my shell.

Chapter
5

On Wednesday, when Mrs. Hastings pulled her silver minivan into my driveway, I called bye to Mom and ran out into the sticky summer air to join Alex in the back seat.

This was my first time leaving the house since the big announcement. Mom hadn't wanted to go anywhere, or even leave the couch. And I hadn't wanted to leave her, so I'd watched as much HGTV as I could stand, exchanged a massive amount of texts with Mackenzie, and scrolled Instagram. I had also done a fair job at ignoring texts from Dad. So far, he'd sent three. All variations of "I'd like to talk."

"Hi, Tessa," Mrs. Hastings greeted me as I climbed in the van.

"Hi. Thanks for picking me up."

Mrs. Hastings put the van in reverse. "Never a problem."

The Hastings family had moved into the house at the end of our street the summer before Alex and I started second grade. When I'd first heard from neighbors that the new family had three boys, I'd been supremely disappointed. But within several weeks, Alex and I were walking to and from school together, along with his brothers, and I no longer wished for the new neighbors to have a daughter. Alex was intelligent, funny, surprisingly thoughtful for a boy, and he didn't mind that I was faster than him in the pool. Probably because he was faster than me on land.

Even with all our history, I felt as awkward being with Alex as I did the first day I wore a bra to school. Like I had changed but nothing else had.

"Tessa, how do you feel about starting school next week? Oh, wait." Mrs. Hastings' ringing cell phone—connected to the van's Bluetooth—filled the van speakers. "Sorry."

Alex hoisted his eyebrows at me. "This is always fun. She can't figure out how to turn on private mode in the van."

"Quiet, you," his mom said good-naturedly. "I have to take this. Please don't embarrass me."

Alex grinned at me, and I was grateful that whoever this Diana was chose to call at this particular moment with her middle school PTA crisis. Their conversation blared over the speakers, limiting Alex's and my freedom to chat. He quietly asked how Mackenzie was doing, and in an attempt to act normal I asked if Cody was home yet, but it was too hard to converse with Diana's shrill, panicked voice in surround sound.

Not that I minded. In a few minutes, we would be at church. Alex would join the boys for small-group time, and I would join the girls. Since Mom always picked me up early for swimming, I would miss the coed time and wouldn't have to work to act normal for the drive home. I kinda wished I had taken Mom's offer to stay home tonight, because this felt exhausting—and the evening had barely begun.

When we pulled into Faith Community Church, Mrs. Hastings waved goodbye to us as she continued to listen to Diana hysterically describe a meeting with the new principal. In addition to Alex, Mrs. Hastings had a senior and a seventh grader; she was nearly impossible to ruffle and kept inserting soothing comments like, "Okay. What else, Diana?"

Alex held the side door to the church open for me. I was about to tell him bye and head off for the girls' lounge when he caught my arm. "Hey, can we talk for a minute?"

His voice was low, and my heart tripped over itself when I looked up at him. "Sure."

Alex ducked in the doorway of a tiny kitchenette off the hallway. We could still be seen, but no one could hear us without obviously lingering.

Alex stared at me for a moment, like he was waiting for me to go first or something. He smoothed his hair, but it just flopped back into place. He had great hair. "Surfer hair," Leilani always gushed when they were dating.

"So." Alex leaned against the counter. "Your mom talked to my mom. About . . . your parents, I mean. I just wanted to tell you how sorry I am."

I sucked in a breath. *My mom was telling people? I guess it made sense. Mackenzie and I had been texting about it for days. And Mrs. Hastings and Mom were friends.*

"Thanks," I said to my flip-flops.

"I just couldn't believe it when Mom told me this afternoon. Did you have any idea?"

A few girls walked by, and I angled away so I wouldn't have to make eye contact. "I don't know."

Alex must've noticed my discomfort because he said in a low voice, "Should we talk later about this? I could call you?"

I nodded and said, "Yeah, I don't really want to talk about it here."

"I get it." Alex straightened. "I wouldn't have brought it up except I was worried."

"Thanks, but it's fine." I took a step sideways, out the doorway. A sea turtle, slipping away. "I'm fine."

Alex just blinked at me, and I pushed a smile onto my face that hopefully looked more normal than it felt and headed down the hall.

When I stepped into the girls' lounge, Izzy bounded up beside me, her wild curls swinging with her. "*Hola*, Tessa!" She hugged me, which I'd learned in the couple of months of our casual friendship was just par for the course. "What's up?"

"Not much. How are you?"

"Great! I saw you talking to Alex when I came in." Izzy's grin had a mischievous tilt to it. "It looked serious."

"Oh, no it wasn't. We were just—" I searched for a better word and came up empty—"talking."

Izzy laughed and twisted her dark hair around a finger. "Well, yeah. I figured that out, thanks."

"I saw your cupcakes on Instagram. They looked good."

"Yeah! I really wanted you to come over. What were you doing?"

Dealing with the dumpster fire of my home life.

Was two months of friendship enough for sharing life-shattering details? Izzy and I had only been friends since June, when she moved to Riverbend from somewhere rural that I could never remember. In many ways, Isabella Valadez was the complete opposite of Mackenzie, April, and Leilani. While the three of them were all about glamour and sophistication, being with Izzy sometimes felt like having an oversized puppy around. Mackenzie and I had run into Izzy once at Taqueria El Rancho, and Mackenzie had giggled about Izzy's unicorn-printed leggings and her wild hair. I probably should've said something to stick up for Izzy. She was a genuinely nice person I enjoyed being around.

Even still, I couldn't make myself say the words, *My parents told me they're getting divorced.*

"I was swimming," I lied instead.

"I should've assumed." Izzy dug through her leather backpack purse. "Oh, that's right. I already checked in my phone. I took videos for IGTV, but our internet has been glitchy."

"Hey, girls." Our small-group leader, Zoe, greeted us by putting arms around each of our shoulders. "How has your week been?"

"*Bueno!* I was just telling Tessa about these cupcakes I baked on Sunday. I was going to show her videos, but I already checked in my phone."

"I think you'll like the prize tonight," Zoe said, referring to the incentive our youth group offered to those who chose to check in their phones before Bible study started.

As Zoe and Izzy talked about the current heat wave, I tried to keep a smile on my face and act normal. *How has your week been?* Such a common question to ask, and yet I felt stumped for how to answer. I didn't want to lie to Zoe. I also didn't want to tell the truth and risk a breakdown in front of everybody.

Maybe Izzy would talk enough for the both of us.

Zoe turned to me with a soft expression. "Could I borrow you for a minute, Tessa?"

Her dark eyes told me before words could. She knew.

"Sure," I said with way too much sunshine in my voice.

"We'll be right back," Zoe said to Izzy, and guided me away, back toward the church offices. They were empty at this time of night, with only a few lights turned on.

Zoe flipped on the light in the youth pastor's office. "Brad said I could use his office for a few minutes so we could talk in private."

"Did my mom call you?"

Zoe nodded and leaned against Brad's desk, and her box braids swung with the motion. "She did, Tessa. I'm just so sorry to hear about what's happened," she said.

I stared at my flip-flops, letting my dark-brown hair fall like curtains around either side of my face. "Yeah. Same."

"My parents are divorced too, and I get it. I know everything looks bleak right now. Can I do anything for you? Do you want to set up a time to go for coffee and talk?"

Zoe had always seemed so cool to me. As one of the few black women in our church, she couldn't help but stand out, and she wore the attention well. I admired that and would normally relish extra time with her. But the idea of being trapped in a conversation about my life put my antiperspirant to work. "I'm fine. I know you're busy with grad school."

"We're all busy, Tessa. I would enjoy getting coffee with you. Whenever you feel ready, okay? I know we need to get to group, but I'm going to pray for you first."

Besides my parents, nobody had ever prayed for me. "Um, okay."

Zoe placed a hand on my shoulder, gave me a sympathetic smile, and bowed her head. "Father God, I raise up my sister Tessa to You. I ask for You to surround her with peace and strength as she walks through this valley. The whole Hart family needs You, Lord. We know You're capable of doing more than we can ever imagine, and I ask that You restore the marriage between Carrie and David."

Restore their marriage. I almost laughed. Had mom not told Zoe about Rebecca?

"Even if that's not the outcome, I trust that You will work out everything for Tessa's good, just like You promise in Your Word. In Jesus' name, amen."

"Thank you," I murmured.

Should I be praying for reconciliation between my parents? Did Mom even want that? She couldn't actually trust Dad again, could she? Trusting him seemed foolish and weak.

"Anytime, Tessa. We could pray as a group, too, if you'd . . ." Zoe trailed off as I shook my head. She smiled and continued, "We certainly don't have to. Whatever you're comfortable with."

"Thanks."

Zoe flipped the light switch in Brad's office. I followed her

out, thinking about those words: *whatever you're comfortable with.*
Nothing about this felt comfortable. The pity. The sympathy. The
prayers. I didn't know the rules here in this place of heartbreak.

I'm the turtle, I told myself. I imagined my clothing—swimsuit,
sky-blue tee, and yoga pants—as my protective shell as I trailed
behind Zoe back to the lounge.

Izzy had claimed our favorite turquoise beanbag chairs by
stretching herself across both. She sat up with a smile when I came
in the room. None of the girls at youth group had ever saved me
a seat before, and it annoyed me that the simple act of friendship
made my eyes misty.

I took the seat with what I hoped was a normal-looking smile
that communicated something along the lines of "Thanks for the
seat, but don't ask what Zoe wanted to talk about."

Izzy said, "What did Zoe want to talk to you about?" with a
brightness in her brown eyes, like she was just sure it was something great.

"Oh, just . . ." Why couldn't I think of *anything*? Surely there
were dozens of reasons that were *not* my parents splitting up that I
could offer to Izzy, but the only thing running through my mind
was the truth.

Izzy cocked her head at me. "Are you okay?"

"Fine. Just . . ." *Turtle. I'm a turtle.* "Nothing. Everything's
good."

Izzy looked unconvinced, and my stomach twisted just enough
to inform me that lying to a friend—even a casual friend—was not
the right thing to do.

Maybe a half-truth would satisfy my conscience. "My parents
are having some problems. That's all."

"Oh, I'm so sorry." Izzy turned from concerned to sympathetic
in an instant. "Like fighting a lot? I hate when my parents fight."

I glanced again at Zoe. She chatted with a girl I recognized
from Northside High, Lauren, rather than starting the Bible study.

"Yeah. Fighting." I looked at Izzy and still felt that pinch of guilt.

"I'm so sorry."

I waved my hand, shaking away her offering of shock and sympathy. "It's okay. It'll all be fine. God's got this, right?"

Did He?

"Of course He does." Izzy's voice was rich with sincerity, as though there wasn't a doubt in her mind. I wished the same could be said for me.

"All right, girls, let's get started," Zoe said about two minutes too late as she took a seat. "This is our last week in the book of James. . . ."

Izzy's hand closed around my arm, and she waited for me to look at her before she said earnestly, "If there's anything I can do, just let me know."

My smile felt like a mask. A shell. "Thanks. I will."

But I wouldn't. Because what could anybody really do to make this better?

—⁓—

April called me as I walked home from swimming later that night. I almost pushed her into voicemail—I was so tired of trying to act normal with people—but that didn't seem like the right thing to do.

"Hey, April."

"Tessa! What are you up to tonight?"

I waved goodbye to Abraham and Lexi. They stood alongside her car, leaning into their conversation in a way that suggested flirting. "Walking home from swimming—"

"Okay, great. Leilani just got a call from Noah asking if we want to hang out. Should we come pick you up?"

"No, thanks. I'm pretty tired." And also, not a fan of Noah.

"What?" April groaned. In the background, I could hear Leilani saying something. "Come on, Tessa. School starts in less than a week! We need to have some fun first."

"I'm really not in the mood, but thanks." April was one of my closest friends. Or she used to be, anyway. I should tell her. She'd be mad if she heard from Mackenzie or Alex. "Actually I just found out my parents are getting divorced, so—"

"What?" This time she screeched the word. "No way. *Your* parents?"

"Yeah."

"Oh, Tess. I'm so sorry." April moved the phone from her mouth and said—presumably to Leilani—"She just found out her parents are getting divorced."

Leilani's, "No!" came through loud and clear.

"What happened?" April spoke into the phone again. "Did you know at the party?"

"No. I had no idea."

Every time I admitted that, it felt like I had failed somehow. Like if only I'd realized things weren't good between them, I could've . . . what? Done something? Stopped it? Saved their marriage?

"Leilani's asking why. Here, I'm just going to put you on speakerphone."

That was, like, the last way I wanted to have this conversation. "Actually, I need to—"

"Okay, you're on speaker." April sounded far away.

"Tessa, I'm soooo sorry," Leilani cooed. "What can we do? Would it help to go out tonight?"

"No, but thanks." I passed a mom pushing a double stroller along the wooded path back to my neighborhood and avoided eye contact. "I want to be with my mom."

"So, she's pretty upset? Was it your dad's choice?"

I wished I'd let the call go to voicemail. I pitched my voice low. "Yeah, my dad has been seeing someone else—"

"No!" they both cried.

"Ugh, *men*," April said venomously. "I never would've thought that of your dad, though. Is she younger?"

"I don't think so. She used to be his girlfriend in high school."

"At least she's not younger," Leilani said. "The girl my dad is dating is only a few years older than me, and it's disgusting."

"What's her name?" April asked. "Have you looked her up on social?"

"No." *Why hadn't I thought to do that yet?* "I guess I should."

"What you should do is come out with us tonight," April said. "It would be good for you. Noah actually just pulled in the driveway. We can come get you next."

I should probably have felt flattered to be invited to hang with a senior like Noah, but I really didn't. I'd never liked him, even before he broke Mackenzie's heart. Now that I thought about it, I felt a little surprised April and Leilani would still hang out with him after that.

"No, I'm exhausted. You two have a good time."

"We're just a text away if you need us," Leilani said, getting progressively closer to the speaker.

"Thanks, girls. I'll talk to you later."

I hung up and saw Dad had texted me while I was on the phone. I'd really like to see you. I'm sure you have lots of questions. I love you.

I put my phone in my bag and hustled the rest of the way home.

At home, Mom was on the couch watching some home renovation show, but she at least had an open bag of microwave popcorn on her lap. Getting herself food was a positive step.

"Hi, Mom."

She paused her show. "Hi, honey. How was your night?"

"Good." I glanced around for evidence that she'd done anything while I was gone. The mail was still piled on the hall table.

The lights were off everywhere except this room. I was willing to bet those towels I'd thrown in the washer earlier were still sitting in the drum. "How about you?"

"I met your friend Izzy just a bit ago. She said she knows you from youth group. She seemed like a nice girl."

"Izzy came by?" I pulled my phone from my bag. *Had I missed a call or something?*

"She brought you cupcakes. They're on the kitchen counter."

I crossed through the living room to find a paper plate with a dozen chocolate cupcakes frosted with peanut butter icing. At a youth event a few weeks before, there had been chocolate cupcakes, and I made a passing comment about chocolate always being better with peanut butter. She'd remembered that.

"Is her family new to Faith Community? I don't remember meeting her before."

"They just moved here from some small town that I can't remember. Her mom's a doctor. I don't remember what her dad does."

I still couldn't take my eyes off the cupcakes. I'd blown off Izzy's sympathy, told her half-truths about my parents, and she'd gone home and baked me cupcakes.

"Well, she seemed very nice. I'm glad to know you have a friend like her. I think that's the only way we're going to get through this season, Tessa."

"Yeah," I answered.

Mom resumed her show. I selected a cupcake and considered my text thread with Izzy.

The cupcakes are amazing, thank you.

I looked at the blinking cursor. I should just leave it at that. No need to say more. I hit Send.

Izzy texted back.

Yay! You just seemed sad and cupcakes make everything better. I'm praying for you, friend!

Guilt nibbled at me as I nibbled on my cupcake. The news would be out in church before too long, if it wasn't already. I didn't want her to hear from someone else.

Thanks. I actually downplayed how bad things are. My dad moved out Sunday. Divorce is looking pretty likely.

Reading over the words, I felt like Tessa the Turtle sticking her head out of her shell. *Is it safe out here?*

I hit Send. It's not like Izzy and me were super-close friends or anything. If she got weird about my parents, I wouldn't lose a lot.

Even still, my knee bounced so much, Mom gave me a look. I stopped.

Mom turned back to the TV. "I think in a couple years, they're going to look at this motif and think, 'Why did we put copper everywhere?'"

"Mm-hmm." As if I had any idea what was going on in the show.

My phone buzzed.

Oh, Tessa! I'm so heartbroken for you. I don't even know what to say, really, but thank you for telling me. You wanna come over tomorrow? I have to babysit Sebastian so can't leave my house. If I hand him his Nintendo Switch, he'll disappear for hours and we can talk. Think about it and let me know. Hugs!

"Who are you texting with?" Mom asked.

That tightness in my chest had eased. I smiled at Mom and said, "My friend Izzy."

Chapter

6

FIRST-DAY-OF-SCHOOL PICTURES had always been a production with Mom. She would pose me on the porch beside oversized flowerpots, holding a chalkboard sign on which she had spent time beautifully hand-lettering the school year and my grade. She fussed with everything—my hair, my clothes, the positioning of my feet—until she felt every detail was right before snapping the picture.

So as she dropped me off in the carpool line that first morning of sophomore year, all I could think was *You didn't take a single picture.*

"Have a good day, honey." Mom's smile looked tired and forced. She had on the same "Run for the arts" 5K T-shirt and yoga pants combination as last night . . . but maybe she was planning to go for a walk after dropping me off?

I pushed away my concerns and headed through the doors of Northside High School, veering right to the office because somehow my request for Intro to Organic Farming had turned into Intro to Drama on my schedule.

Um, NO.

Mrs. James, the school receptionist, was already helping another student sort out a schedule situation, so I got in line and reached into my backpack for my own printed copy.

"Tessa! What's up?"

I turned to see Izzy seated in one of the office chairs, her phone on her lap. "What are you doing in here?"

"Waiting for my 'school ambassador' to arrive." Izzy hung air quotes around the phrase we used to describe a student who showed another student the ropes on their first day.

"Who is it?"

"Amelia . . . something. Bryan, maybe?"

"Oh! Millie Bryan?" Millie's face came to mind immediately, round and smiling with her thick, red-gold hair frizzing around her face. "You'll like her. She's very friendly."

Millie and I weren't friends, really, but she was impossible to not notice. She was a bigger girl, though she never seemed self-conscious about her extra weight. Or if she did, it didn't keep her out of the spotlight. She did everything slightly louder than I would ever dare—humming to herself in the hallways, conversations with friends that the whole class could listen in on, color choices for clothes.

"Were you waiting for me?" Mrs. James called, and I turned.

"Yes, Mrs. James. There's been a mix-up in my schedule." I slid the paper across to her. "I never signed up for Intro to Drama. This was supposed to be Organic Farming," I said, tapping the offending entry.

"Okay." Mrs. James clicked a few times on her computer. "Remind me of your name, honey."

"Tessa Hart. H-A-R-T."

"There you are, Tessa." More clicking. "That organic farming class is so popular, I doubt there will be any room left."

"But I signed up for it in the spring."

"I know, but clearly that's not what the system logged. You might have to try again next semester." Mrs. James leaned close to her screen and her oversized hoop earrings fell forward too. "Yep, full. Now, do you want to stay with Intro to Drama or should I look at what else is available?"

"Ooh, Tessa!" Izzy materialized at my shoulder. "Stay in Drama! I'm taking it too."

"No way. I don't know anything about drama."

Izzy giggled. "That's why it's *Intro* to Drama, silly."

"You do need a fine-arts credit before you graduate," Mrs. James pointed out oh so helpfully. "Drama would fill that."

"What else could I take?"

The office door swung open and Millie charged in, out of breath, her rainbow-colored cardigan streaming behind her. "Sorry I'm late!" She looked from me to Izzy. "You must be Isabella."

"German I?" Mrs. James suggested.

I huffed a humorless laugh. "No, thanks. I already take French."

"So that's a no to Spanish I as well?"

"What about photography or graphic design? Something else that would fill fine arts?"

She clicked a few times and I tried not to eavesdrop on Millie and Izzy's conversation. Millie tended to speak in exclamations, however, so it was difficult to not listen in as she explained that she was late because she'd left her phone at home and had to go back to get it.

"Photography is full and graphic design is only available second period." Mrs. James folded her hands together and looked up at me expectantly. "Study hall?"

"I have a study hall already during sixth period."

"Would you like another?"

I resisted rolling my eyes. Only slackers took two study halls. I didn't even like taking one, but it was helpful with how busy swimming kept me in the evenings.

Izzy grabbed hold of my arm. "Amelia is in Intro to Drama too! She says it's really fun and you'll love it."

"Ms. Larkin is ah-mazing." Millie sang the last word before launching into a rapid-fire explanation. "I actually already took intro last year, so I'm also taking Drama II, but Ms. Larkin approved me to be a teacher's assistant of sorts for Drama I. It's going to be the absolute best, Tessa. Seriously, you have to take it."

"But I can't act."

Not that I had tried recently—or ever—but I was pretty sure that was true. Even on days that I gave oral presentations, I could barely eat breakfast. Teachers always wrote comments about my good information but my lack of vibrancy as a speaker.

Millie waved this away. "Of course you can. Everybody can act. We just need to unleash you." She made a sweeping gesture with her hands when she said *unleash you*. As if she intended to revamp my whole self.

I must've made a face—I didn't want to be "unleashed," thank you very much—because Millie laughed and said a more earnest "You won't regret taking it, Tessa. I promise."

"Okay, Miss Hart," Mrs. James prompted. "I need a decision so I can help these other students. Keep you in Drama or switch you to study hall?"

I glanced at the line that had formed behind me. I couldn't justify taking two study halls when Intro to Drama would knock out my fine-arts requirement. And Izzy would be in there.

"Fine," I said with a sigh. "Keep me in Drama."

Izzy cheered and squeezed me with an unnecessary celebratory hug. Millie clapped with such gusto, you would've thought we were actually good friends and this was some huge victory for her.

"I better not regret this," I grumbled to both of them.

—◈—

Spotting the back of Alex's sandy-blond head in Honors English was the first good thing that had happened that day. After a hitch of hesitation, I slid into the seat beside him with a soft "Hey."

"Oh, hi." He put his phone to sleep, but I caught a glimpse of his Instagram feed before the screen went dark. "Sorry I missed your call last night. I was babysitting for my cousin and couldn't answer. I tried calling back."

"Yeah, I saw. I was on the phone with Mackenzie."

"Oddly, I was just looking at Mackenzie's Insta post." Alex's knee bounced beneath his desk. "I'm thinking I need to move to Florida."

I snorted. "Yeah, I bet."

I'd also seen Mackenzie's post. Sunset pictures on the beach, where she and her cousins and some of their friends had set up a movie night with hammocks. The whole scene looked like something you would see on a TV show, complete with unrealistically pretty girls. The magic of filters. Even Mackenzie looked more radiant than I remembered. *Or were Florida girls just prettier than Indiana girls?*

Alex frowned at my tone. "Not because of . . . well . . . I mean . . . just the idea of watching a movie on the beach is pretty sweet."

"Mm-hmm. Sure."

Alex sat up and his leg stopped vibrating. "I definitely don't mean because of her friends."

I smirked. "Who said you did?"

Alex's eyes sparked. "You maybe didn't use words, but I've known you long enough to pick up on your subtext, Tessa Rae."

I opened my mouth to respond when Lauren from our youth group slid into the seat behind Alex. "Hey, guys, how's it going?"

Her friendly smile startled me. Not that Lauren was unfriendly, just that I couldn't recall a time that she greeted me so warmly.

Alex turned and rested his elbow on her desk. "Good, how about you?"

She tucked long strands of honey-blond hair behind her ears and looked at him through lowered lashes. A strange, irrational flash of jealousy zipped through me. I'd seen that look plenty last year when Leilani was into Alex.

I turned away and pulled out my phone.

"Fine, now that I'm done taking all those first-day-of-school pictures," Lauren said with a laugh. "My dad still wants me to pose by the school sign, like I'm in elementary school or something."

"My brother's a senior, so my mom was kind of a weepy mess this morning." Alex turned to me. "What about you? Was your mom her usual crazy self with the pictures?"

"Yeah," I said, not daring to look at him. "Totally."

Lauren brought up a basketball camp they'd apparently both been at this summer, leaving me free to ignore them without being rude. I swiped away a new text from Dad—Hope you have a great first day of school! What do you say to dinner tonight?—and pulled up Rebecca's Instagram profile.

When I first looked her up a few days ago, I thought I must have the wrong Rebecca Simmons, because she had over 25,000 followers. Apparently, Dad's new girlfriend had some level of Instagram fame among elementary teachers who liked looking at classroom setups and bulletin-board displays. I didn't want to actually follow her—though would she even notice with how many she had?—but I also couldn't seem to stop peeking at her account. Especially because she posted multiple times a day in addition to posting a story, so there was always something new.

Her newest photo was an artsy black-and-white selfie of her and my dad, with their cheeks pressed against each other's and their eyes squinting slightly as they smiled for the shot. Like always, my dad was looking in slightly the wrong spot, but Rebecca was a pro and knew how to look into the lens.

Me and my guy at the Riverbend Pottery Festival, the caption read.

The words sucked all the air from my lungs. I clicked to read more, even though as it was, I could barely breathe. I skimmed details of their festival experience, and then, because apparently I had self-destructive tendencies, began to read through the comments.

> Linzy2545: you two are adorbs
> RebeccaLovesToTeach: thanks! He's a keeper!

I put my phone to sleep, but I couldn't turn off Dad's big smile and Rebecca's big words. He had been somebody else's "keeper" until she came along.

"You okay?"

I opened my eyes to find Alex's face creased in concern. Lauren watched me too, still leaning forward on her desk, closer to Alex than necessary.

"Yeah, fine."

"You sure? Because—"

"I said I'm fine." The words snapped out of me, and I could see the same surprise I felt on both their faces. Heat bloomed in my cheeks. "I'm sorry, I didn't mean to say it like that."

"No, that's okay." Alex looked hurt, and he angled his knees back under his desk.

I told myself it didn't matter if I'd hurt his feelings. Hadn't he hurt my feelings dozens of times in the last year while I watched him pursue Leilani?

"I'm really sorry," I said again as the bell rang.

He waved away the apology. "It's no big deal. I'm glad you're fine."

As Mr. Huntley began the first class of my sophomore year, I wondered if any statement could be less true.

—⁂—

Instead of a room number for Intro to Drama, my schedule said *MUL. What did that mean?* My stomach growled, I had a dull ache in the nape of my neck, and I still couldn't get Rebecca's *He's a keeper!* out of my head, so I was already in what my mother would call "a mood." Now I had to figure out where this stupid class was without the aid of a room number.

I closed my locker door with a bit more force than necessary and surveyed my hallway options. Most art classes were on the lower level, near the office, so . . .

I heard Millie Bryan's loud laugh, and then caught sight of her thick, reddish hair. And that was definitely Izzy loping alongside her. There were too many students between us for me to catch up to them, but I kept them in sight most of the way. I turned into the hall just as they disappeared into a doorway for the multipurpose room. If I hadn't been hungry, headachy, and seething over what I'd seen on Instagram, I probably would've had the brainpower to put together what *MUL* could be short for.

As soon as I opened the door and stepped into the room, I wanted to back out and run immediately.

To my left was the stage, just a few steps up from the ground. It was smaller than the one in the auditorium, but terrifying none-theless. Millie stood in the middle of it, gesturing grandly as she gave a tour to wide-eyed Izzy.

They were the only ones on the stage. The rest of the students mingled awkwardly around what looked like some sort of living-room graveyard of secondhand love seats and wingback chairs in various clashing patterns and colors. There were a variety of bean-bag chairs scattered around the rug as well, and a chair as tall as me that was hot pink and shaped like a high-heel shoe.

The only desk I saw was in the back of the room, where Ms. Larkin sat now, poking at something on her iPad. Other than Millie and Izzy, I didn't recognize a single student in here.

"Welcome to Drama I, kiddos!" Ms. Larkin called as she stood from her desk. "Please silence your phone and put them in the organizer by the door, and then choose a seat on the rug anywhere you'd like."

Mounted on the wall by the door was a shoe organizer with see-through sleeves. I recognized Izzy's phone case with a cartoon of some man on it and put mine beside hers. By the time I turned around and surveyed seating options, Millie and Izzy had claimed a black-and-white-striped love seat. Izzy waved and patted a non-existent spot beside her.

I rolled my eyes. "How little do you think I am?" I asked as I drew near. "There's, like, three inches of space there."

"We can make room." Millie scooched against the arm of the love seat.

I took a spot on the thick, charcoal-colored rug. "I'm fine on the floor, thanks."

Ms. Larkin stood near the stage, watching all of us with a smile. I'd noticed her before at various all-school events because she was always dressed so prettily, in flowing skirts and blousy tops. It was a kind of style that made me think, *When I'm in my thirties, that's how I'd like to dress.* Today her skirt was olive green, and her blouse pale pink and sleeveless. The way she beamed at us all, as if already pleased, gave me a stab of longing for Ms. Larkin to like me.

"We are going to have so much fun in here, I just can't wait. Every day when you come in, I want the first thing you do to be silencing or turning off your phones and putting them in the organizer by the door. This room is a special space within the school walls. A sacred space. It's important that we disconnect from what's *outside* the classroom so that we can connect better *within* the classroom. Yes?"

My stomach squirmed. These weren't the kind of spiels you got in a real class. Mrs. Parks hadn't claimed the chemistry lab was "sacred." I glanced around. Some students looked as freaked out as I felt. A few seemed to have already zoned out. But about half—Millie and Izzy included—wore the wide-eyed, eager-to-please faces of people who had purposefully signed up for drama class.

Ms. Larkin spent about ten minutes going over the need-to-know information. That our big project this first semester was a one-act play that we would start in September and perform in groups. We would each spend some time learning basics about lighting and set design. To get an A in her class, she needed to see us putting forth effort and being willing to grow in our abilities.

Ms. Larkin set her iPad on a nearby end table and clapped her hands together. "Now that we have all that out of the way, let's do something fun. Let's get into groups of three."

"Me too, Ms. Larkin?" Millie called out.

Ms. Larkin gave Millie a warm smile that made me feel a zip of jealousy. "Yes, you too."

I glanced at Millie and Izzy and found them already looking at me, only their expressions looked as if they might burst with the excitement of it all. At least finding a group was easy.

As students shuffled about in the room to get in their groups, Ms. Larkin's voice rose above the noise, "We're going to play Two Truths and a Lie. I imagine you know how to play, but you will tell your other group members three things about yourselves. Two of them should be true, one should be a lie. The object is to tell a lie disguised as truth. And to have fun."

"I'll go first," Millie and Izzy said simultaneously. They looked at each other and laughed.

"Go ahead," Millie said.

"Okay." Izzy drew her knees up to her chest, wrapped her arms around her glittery black leggings, and grinned at us both before saying, "I'm the youngest in my family. I was born in Mexico. And my first kiss was a dolphin."

"You are *not* the youngest in your family," I said. "Sebastian is."

"Oh, stars. I forgot you've met him at church."

"Even without knowing your brother, that would've been my guess too," Millie said in a teachery-type voice. "You chose two unique details and then one ordinary detail, but the trick with Two Truths and a Lie is to pick all ordinary facts. Like: I prefer to be called Amelia. My brother got married this summer. My favorite ice cream is cookie dough."

"Oh, you're right." Izzy's voice had an awed quality. "It *is* much harder like this. Did your brother actually get married this summer?"

Millie nodded with a self-satisfied smile that definitely didn't improve my irritable state. Somebody was really impressed with herself for being a TA. "He did," she sighed.

Until Izzy called her Amelia this morning, I'd never heard her referred to in that way. "Do you actually prefer Amelia?"

"I do. But my favorite ice cream is mint chocolate chip. Not cookie dough."

"That was so smart, Amelia," Izzy said, pulling strands of her curling hair through her fingers.

Izzy's admiration made me want to think of really obscure, exotic facts about myself just to prove Millie wrong about the "best" way to play Two Truths and a Lie. Unfortunately, my life wasn't very exotic.

They both looked at me, and I felt sweaty. Izzy began to braid the strands of hair she'd separated. Ms. Larkin had begun drifting around the room and would probably wind up at our group soon.

"Um, okay." I tucked my hair behind my ears. "I've never had a pet. My favorite constellation is Cassiopeia, and . . ." I needed a lie . . . needed a lie . . . needed a lie. "I've only moved once."

"That's the lie," Millie—Amelia, rather—said with a soft laugh, like a parent finding amusement with a child's attempts. "Those were good facts, Tessa, but you'll need to be smoother in your delivery if you want to be convincing. I'm sure you'll do better next time."

I swallowed the snarky response sitting on my tongue and made myself say, "Thanks."

Izzy dropped her miniature braid and clapped her hands. "Let's play again!"

Maybe this time I would pick, "I think Drama will be fun," as my lie.

Chapter

7

WHEN MOM PICKED ME UP FROM SCHOOL wearing different clothes—a running tank and shorts—my mood boosted. She still didn't have on makeup, and she hardly asked me any questions on the way home, but at least she changed her clothes at some point while I was at school.

When we got home, however, my optimism plummeted. Many of the curtains were still drawn, and the house smelled like the kitchen trash was overdue to be taken out. If anything, it appeared as though Mom had backslid today.

"What kind of cereal do you want?" I called from the kitchen as I pulled back a few curtains and let the sunlight in.

"What?" Mom's voice came from the living room.

I leaned through the doorway. My mom was already back on the couch, pulling a throw around her shoulders even though it was ninety degrees outside. Her expression was blank, like she'd completely forgotten the tradition we'd had since kindergarten of sugary cereals for our after-school snack.

"What kind of cereal do you want?" I repeated, trying to keep my voice light.

"Oh. I don't know. Do we have any?"

How would I know? I wasn't the one who did the grocery shopping.

"I'll check." I turned toward the pantry and winced when the TV flicked on. In the last week and a half, Mom had watched more TV than I'd seen her watch in my entire life.

"There's Cap'n Crunch," I called to Mom, scanning the coordinated cereal storage containers. "And enough Cookie Crisp for one."

"I'm not very hungry. Just have what you want, Tessa."

I ran my hand over the granite counters. Very clean. Almost like she hadn't been in here today. "What did you have for lunch?"

A beat of silence fell. "An apple. And some cheese, too."

I crossed to the doorway and gave her a pointed look.

She sighed. "I'm just not hungry. I had to talk to your dad today."

My brain lit up with that black-and-white photo of him on Instagram. His cheek against Rebecca's. The soft smile. *He's a keeper!* "Why?"

"Because he said he's been trying to get ahold of you and you're not responding. He wants to take you out to dinner tonight."

My body felt the same as the time Mom made me eat liver. Like everything on the inside of my stomach wanted to be on the outside of my stomach. So she'd backslid because of me. Because I wasn't responding to Dad, and he'd pushed the issue. "I don't want to do that."

Mom sighed. "I thought that might be your reaction." Mom folded her hands on her lap. "And I definitely understand it. But at the end of the day, he *is* your father—"

"Who walked out on us not even two weeks ago."

"Yes, that's true."

"I'm not going out with him and Rebecca. I'm not pretending what he did is totally fine."

"He said it would be just the two of you. And nobody is asking you to pretend anything."

"Just sitting there would be pretending."

A ghost of a smile passed over Mom's face. "What would you be pretending by sitting there?"

"That things are okay."

"Your dad knows things aren't okay. That's why he wants to go out to dinner. To start working on making things better."

"I'm not going to leave you here all night on the couch, eating nothing and watching TV."

Mom ducked her head, looking slightly ashamed. "I'll be fine here. I'm just going through an adjustment."

Not very well.

I swept away the judgmental thoughts. I'd never even had a boyfriend; how could I really understand what it must feel like to have your husband of seventeen years leave you for his first love?

Even still, a steady diet of mindless television and not showering didn't seem like healthy coping. There was nothing to force her out of the house, other than picking me up, and she could do that from the privacy of her car. I wished she had a real job—the "nine-to-five at an office wearing a pencil skirt" kind of job—that would force her to go somewhere that felt normal without my dad.

I sat on the edge of the couch, down by her feet. "I know it's hard." I tried to keep my voice as light and kind as possible. "But I'm worried about you."

Mom's attempt at a reassuring smile was short-lived. "I know. I'm grieving. But I'll come out on the other side of this. When I lost your Nana, I was like this for a week or so, and then I was able to put the pieces of life back together. It's just part of my process."

Mom's mom had died when I was in fourth grade. I remembered my own piercing sadness, but not much about my mom's sorrow.

"I understand needing to grieve," I said, still trying to keep my voice gentle. "It just seems like if you tried to add in something normal that got you out of the house, it would help."

"Do you know what God gave us feelings for?"

"Uh . . ."

"To *feel* them. We're not supposed to ignore them or analyze them or judge them. We're meant to feel our feelings. It's fine to feel sad, Tessa. There's no right or wrong way to feel." Mom blew a long, gray-streaked strand from her face and the mental image of Rebecca's profile picture with her vibrant, auburn hair flashed in my mind. "Sorry. I'm just . . ."

When Mom didn't finish, I volunteered, "Sad?"

She nodded at her hands and said, "Yes. And disgusted. And hurt."

"Me too."

"And angry."

"Yep."

There was a moment of silence and then Mom said, "And I think it's fine for you to express that to your dad tonight over dinner. You can tell him you're feeling all those things."

"I really don't want to go to dinner." My voice sounded whiny, and I hated it.

Mom pulled the cable-knit throw tighter around her shoulders. "I don't like this either, but this is our reality. You will have to see him sometime, either willingly or because a judge says you have to. You love your dad. You can't be angry with him forever."

"Maybe I can. Let's find out."

The corner of Mom's mouth lifted. "I suppose you *could* be angry, but the resentment isn't good for you. I love you too much to want you to hate your dad forever."

"What happened to 'feelings are meant to be felt'? I feel angry, and I feel like I don't want to go to dinner."

"Well, that doesn't mean feelings get to be the boss. There are many, *many* things I feel like doing for revenge against your dad and Rebecca. I'm not doing them. I feel the feelings, and I give them to God." She scrolled through something on her phone. "And then I watch a remodeling show."

I folded my arms over my chest. "But yet I have to feel my feelings and still go out to dinner?"

Mom sighed. "I'm asking you to do it for you. Not for him. For you."

A wry laugh coughed out of me. "Why?"

"Because I love you." Mom seemed to choke on the simple sentence. "You won't be able to heal if you just continue shoving the feelings away, shoving *him* away. You think your anger is keeping him on the hook, but ultimately, it's going to keep you on the hook too. So please go. I think it's the right thing for you to do."

I let a defiant silence hang between us.

"That's really, really unfair of you."

Because she knew "the right thing to do" was an argument that nearly always worked with me. I thundered upstairs and almost slammed my door, but I didn't. It's not like Dad was here to hear it.

—⟋⟍—

When Dad arrived, he pulled his Jeep Cherokee into the driveway and let the engine idle.

I watched from one of the guest-bedroom windows as minutes ticked by. *How long would he sit there waiting to be seen? Would he come to the door? Text me?* But no, he stayed in the safety of his SUV for three minutes before he gave the horn a tentative beep.

"Tessa!" Mom called from the living room. "Dad's here!"

I threw my purse over my shoulder and clomped downstairs.

Mom offered a forced smile from the couch. "Out of habit, I want to say, 'Have a good time.' That doesn't feel very appropriate."

I wanted to glare and fume, but her jaw trembled. Something about how she had the throw wrapped around her made her look small and childlike. I had this strange, warped sensation that I was the adult in the room, and as such, I needed to be the leader.

"I'll be home soon," I said. "Please eat something."

I pulled the front door closed behind me, feeling unexpected guilt. She was the one who pushed me to go. Why should I feel guilty leaving her alone?

I avoided looking at Dad as I walked to the car, keeping my eyes on my turquoise flip-flops. Once again, my anger with him felt like a living, breathing creature residing behind my rib cage.

I popped open the passenger door of the Jeep and climbed in. "Hi, honey."

I pulled the seat belt across my lap. "Hi."

"Thanks for saying yes to dinner."

"Mom made me." That was rude, and I didn't even care.

"Ah, I see. Well." Dad took an audible breath. "Would you like to do this another night? I don't want to force you."

"It's fine." I couldn't just walk back inside the house without getting a lecture from Mom or it turning into one more piece of stress and sadness for her. "Let's just go."

There was such a long silence that I finally broke and looked at him. He appeared to be the man I'd adored all my life—shiny head, blue work shirt, slacks—and yet being with him felt like being with a stranger. *Did he feel that way when he looked at me?*

Dad reached and gave my leg a stiff pat. "What do you feel like for dinner?"

Just the thought of food made me want to throw up; I was so nervous. "I don't care."

"Mexican, Italian, Chinese?"

I nearly said, *Whatever you want,* and then decided that the last thing I wanted tonight was to give Dad more of the things he wanted.

"How about Taqueria El Rancho?" I said. Dad liked the fancier Mexican place in town, but I'd always been partial to the quaintness of Taqueria.

"Great. Taqueria El Rancho it is." Dad infused his voice with enthusiasm, as if he single-handedly could make up for my lack thereof. "I haven't been there in months."

He started the Jeep and backed out of the driveway. I wondered if Mom was crying. Or if there was any chance of her eating tonight.

"How was your first day of school?"

"Fine."

"Do you have any fun classes this semester?"

"Not really."

"Do you have many classes with April and Leilani?"

"None, actually."

"That's too bad."

I shrugged. I hadn't heard from them since last Wednesday when I told them about my parents, and it bugged me. After sharing news like that, was it so wrong to hope a friend might check in on me a time or two?

When the conversation lagged, I noticed the music. Worship music. Not just worship music, but a song that often made me tear up when we sang it at church, about God being with me even when I felt as though I was being battered by waves. Hearing the song in this context—with my cheating father, who drove here from his new home with the woman he left me and Mom for— made the angry beast residing in my ribs seethe.

"I saw Grandma and Grandpa today," Dad said after several more fruitless questions. "Grandma had a real bad cold last week. Did you know that?"

"No."

"I bet it would cheer her up to hear from you."

What had they said about the impending divorce? Had they just found out today, or was this a follow-up conversation? Should I ask?

I was still debating when Dad turned into a small parking lot near the strip of old buildings that was downtown Riverbend. I usually liked the chance to be in this part of town. Whenever we came here for dinner as a family, we would always cruise through Booked Up or Paprika's or one of the other cute shops. Tonight, I just wanted things over as fast as possible.

"Looks pretty busy," Dad said as we drew near the restaurant.

"Mm-hmm."

Dad's sigh was quiet, but I still caught it. *Was he feeling a little annoyed? A little regretful that he'd invited me out? Great. Hopefully it meant he wouldn't ask a second time.*

He held the door open for me, and I stepped into the small entryway, crowded with families of overexcited kids and harried parents.

I expected the hostess to say we had a wait ahead of us. Instead she said a bright "Oh, just two? Right this way."

We sidestepped the families of four and five and followed the hostess to our tiny round table.

"Your server will be right with you," she said, then turned and hurried away.

Dad smiled at me as we took our seats, and then asked, "Do you go to school with her?"

"No, why?"

"She looks about your age. I thought maybe you knew her."

"I don't." I pretended to peruse the menu. Pretended I didn't always order the chicken flautas.

"When I was in high school in Riverbend, everybody knew everybody." Dad opened his menu as well, maybe also looking for a distraction. "I forget sometimes it's not like that anymore."

What would we do after we ordered, when there were no

menus to distract us from each other? It was bad enough in the car, but here we would actually have to face each other while we forced conversation.

"Hey, neighbor."

My head snapped at the sound of Alex's voice. He wore the red polo shirt of all Taqueria El Rancho employees and set bowls of chips and salsa between Dad and me.

"You work here?"

Could I have asked a dumber question?

"Yeah, just started last week." He turned a smile to my father, but it was Alex's polite smile. Not the warm one he'd given me. "Hey, Mr. Hart. Nice to see you."

"You too, Alex. How's your family?"

"Doing great, thanks."

Alex wasn't the type to be rude, but still I didn't like him exchanging pleasantries with my dad.

"What can I bring you two to drink?"

"Just water for me, thanks," Dad said.

"Lemonade, please."

"Sure thing. I'll let you look over the menu a minute longer, and I'll be back to take your order." Alex walked away but flashed me a private thumbs-up. He used to do the same thing in elementary school whenever I had to give any kind of oral presentation, because he knew how nervous they made me. That I would practice obsessively, not wanting to get a single word wrong. The unexpected sign of camaraderie made me blush behind my menu.

"So," I said to Dad, "what are you ordering?"

Dad's smile softened at the first conversation I'd initiated. Stupid Alex for thawing me out.

"My usual." He closed his menu. "The flautas. What about you?"

Why did the flautas never grow old to my dad, but Mom did?

I laid down my menu as well. "Same."

"Now that Alex is working here, maybe he can tell us how they make their chile sauce."

"Yeah, maybe."

My eyes scanned the restaurant for Alex. A middle-aged woman was saying something very long-winded, and Alex nodded as he wrote notes in his order pad.

Dad stacked our menus on the edge of the table. "So I booked our final hotel in Iceland today."

"Oh."

"Oh?"

I shifted in my seat, unsticking my bare legs from the vinyl chair cover. "I'm just not as excited about Iceland as I was."

Dad's face softened. "I know, kiddo. The timing on this is just terrible."

The timing he decided? "Maybe we should put it off, then." The beast twirled inside me. "Or not go at all."

Hurt swept over my dad's face. "Well." Dad dragged out the word. "October is a couple of months from now. You might feel differently—"

Alex swooped back into the conversation, placing our drinks in front of us.

"Do you guys know what you want?"

"I'll have the chicken flauta dinner," Dad said with a forced smile. "Extra chile sauce."

Suddenly the thought of saying, "I'll have the same," felt like some sort of betrayal to my mother. I glanced at the menu on the edge of the table and blurted the first not-flauta dinner I saw, "And I'll have chile rellenos, please."

Alex nodded, unaware that anything unusual had happened. "All right, you two." He gathered our menus and continued, "I'll have those out to you as soon as possible."

As Alex walked away, Dad dug a chip into the salsa. "Change your mind about the flautas?"

And from that snarling beast residing behind my rib cage came, "That's okay, right? To commit to one thing, and then change my mind because something else sounded better in the moment?"

Dad stopped mid-bite, the chip hanging halfway in his mouth. He lowered it and leveled a somber gaze at me. "I know you're very upset with me, Tessa."

I looked away, into my lemonade, and let the heavy maracas of the piped-in music fill the silence between us. I didn't want to get into this now. Not in my favorite restaurant. Not when Alex might see or hear. Not anywhere.

Dad leaned forward. "I don't like this. I don't like never talking to or seeing you."

Looking at his face, so open and somber, sympathy tugged at my heart. But he was the last person who deserved sympathy in this situation. "This was your choice."

Dad, to his credit, agreed. "It was."

Dad's think-it-through nature made this whole cheating and divorce business even worse, because Dad always thought things through. That's why he was always early for events, because he built in time for possible traffic, construction, wrong turns, or all three. Dad must've considered that this choice could irreparably damage our relationship, could mean no Iceland trip, and he'd chosen Rebecca anyway.

"You knew I might react like this." The words held more of an accusing tone than I expected. I was realizing that all those times Dad told me nothing was more important to him than our family, he was totally lying.

"I did, but I didn't think it would be *this* bad."

I swallowed the emotion that rose in my throat. *Hey, turtle. Retreat into your shell. Don't let him see.* "You miscalculated."

He nodded. Finally, he ate that chip that he'd been holding since Alex left.

I took a chip and snapped it into fragments. I wished I could do the same with my pain. Just break it off and brush it onto the floor.

I seared Dad with my gaze. "If you knew that I could never see you the same way again, that to go to Iceland with you now sounds like some kind of prison sentence, would you still have made the same choice?"

Dad shifted. "I'm not sure that's a fair question. The pain is still fresh now. I think over time—"

"If you knew all that—" I tried to hold eye contact, but that was impossible when he wouldn't look at me—"would you still have picked her?"

Dad's hands laced together on the table. "I have to think this part will get better. Lots of parents divorce and—"

"Would you just answer the question?"

He looked at me and stayed silent. *A confirmation if I ever saw one.*

I pushed back from the table. Tears blurred my vision, and I nearly knocked over a waiter as I barreled toward the bathroom. "Sorry," I muttered and kept going.

I slid the bathroom lock into place and paced around the tiny stall, my heart beating as if I'd just swam a 100 butterfly. Even knowing our relationship might be forever ruined—was certainly forever altered—Dad would've picked Rebecca. That truth sliced deep and made the angry creature in my chest stomp around and breathe fire. I stomped around with it for a few minutes until someone else came into the bathroom. Then I emerged and used a damp paper towel to dab at the ring of mascara and eyeliner that I'd cried away.

I fixed my face into a mask of stone and stared at myself in the mirror. Dad had made his choice, and I couldn't change it. But I wasn't going to walk back out to the table looking all devastated. I would muscle my way through dinner and never say yes to this again.

When I marched back out to our tiny table, the surface was crowded with steaming plates and Styrofoam boxes.

"I thought you might be ready to call it a night," Dad said quietly.

And since he offered me the easy way out, I took it. I scraped what was apparently chile rellenos into a box, latched the lid, and stormed outside.

I didn't even respond to his goodbye when I slid out of the Jeep.

Inside, Mom was curled on the couch, eating a bowl of ice cream and watching some black-and-white movie. She wasn't crying now, but her eyes were red and puffy. They widened with shock when I came in. "How'd it go?"

"I was barely gone forty-five minutes," I called over my shoulder as I stalked up the stairs. "How do you think it went?"

This time, I slammed my bedroom door.

—m—

I awoke at 10:30 to my phone buzzing with a new text. Alex's smiling picture hung next to the words: You okay? Dinner looked rough.

I blew out an exhale and studied the screen. Following up was a classic-nice-Alex move. "Why couldn't he like *me*, God? Why'd he have to like Leilani?"

Of course, I knew why he liked Leilani. Her arrival last September was like having a Hawaiian Barbie doll dropped into our Indiana high school. Nobody would've picked me—brown hair, brown eyes, not a single exotic trait to offer—in a beauty contest against Leilani. I just hadn't known Alex was that superficial.

Fine, I texted back. Thanks for checking.

Not that the only thing Leilani offered was a pretty face. Yeah, she was a little ditzy, but she was nice and could be funny sometimes. If she'd been fixated on a different boy, I probably would've liked her just fine. That's what Mackenzie had told me.

"I told you, you should've snapped Alex up when you had the chance," she'd said. Not that my being Alex's official girlfriend would've been any kind of protection. I mean, Mom had been Dad's *wife* and he'd still broken his marriage vows. Could you ever really trust somebody with your heart?

A new message from Alex popped up. Okay. If you want to talk, I'm here.

Of all my friends, he'd been the most attentive about the divorce. Well, him and Izzy. I could tell Mackenzie was over talking about it. She'd started high school in Palm Beach and seemed to think I should be adjusted to the divorce by now.

Thanks.

I studied the word on my screen. It looked cold and dismissive all by itself, and that's not what I wanted. Alex really was a good guy. Logically, I knew it wasn't his fault that he'd had feelings for Leilani and not me.

I hated emojis, but maybe that would soften the single word. When I couldn't find an emoji that seemed suitable, I finally just added my new mantra.

I'm fine.

I should've just turned off my phone and gone back to sleep, but I scrolled my Insta feed instead.

Izzy had made herself an ice cream sundae that matched her ice-cream-sundae pajama pants. Her grinning face made me smile too.

Mackenzie posted the view from her new room, complete with palm trees and an orange sunset. #nofilter, she bragged.

Zoe was fostering a new puppy, and the photo was of her pressing her bright red lips against the dog's squishy face.

Abraham had a fire in his backyard with other students from the prestigious Providence Day School to celebrate the first day of sophomore year.

Lauren—who I hadn't even realized I followed on Instagram—was testing out new lip gloss shades. I watched her Instagram story where she bemoaned stopping by Starbucks to mark surviving the first day of school, and the barista misheard her name and wrote Laura on the cup.

Boo. Hoo. Hoo.

Why was everybody's life so much better than mine? So much easier?

I pulled up Rebecca's profile on Instagram. The newest post was a beautifully designed image of her fall bucket list that I, too, could download if I went to her website. I rolled my eyes at the screen for nobody's benefit but my own, and then clicked so I could read about her desires to bake pumpkin bread and walk down a leaf-covered trail. Her caption of the photo began, "I believe in living a life worth sharing."

I was tempted to click *Read More*, but that would be dumb. I needed sleep, not to torture myself with Rebecca's super-together, share-worthy life.

I turned off my phone and chucked it onto my nightstand. I stared up at my ceiling, the bright-white screen of my phone still burned in my vision.

A life worth sharing. Yeah, it was obvious she thought we all needed to see every detail of her life. And that we wanted all her tips on making our lives just as perfect as hers.

I hadn't posted since Mackenzie's party, because what on earth would I have shared? I had no palm trees out my window. No puppy. No firepit with friends. My post would be something like **Here's the cold chile rellenos that I'm eating alone in my bedroom because I learned my dad would rather be with his new girlfriend than be on speaking terms with me.**

Oh, yeah. That would definitely grow my following.

Meanwhile, people ate up everything Rebecca fed them. Her followers had grown by two hundred this week alone. Two hundred! Which was stupid, because she was really just this ordinary teacher who'd destroyed my family. This in contrast to my mother, who made beautiful artwork and taught popular art classes in our basement, but had seven followers and hadn't even uploaded a profile picture because she just "didn't see the point" of social media.

I'd vowed to Dad that we would be fine without him, but maybe "fine" wasn't enough. Maybe he needed to see we were thriving around here. Maybe it needed to be clear to him that we were living our best, most share-worthy lives without him. And maybe then he would realize what he'd given up and could have back if he only asked.

Maybe if I faked thriving long enough, it would become real.

Chapter
8

"Everything we do in Drama I is the best," Millie said as she, Izzy, and I went through the lunch line together. "You're going to love all of it. The One Acts, the monologues, the improv. Everything is great."

Lunch followed Drama, and Millie had seemed excited for the three of us to sit together. That was fine. April and Leilani had a different lunch period anyway, and Alex, Michael, and Cody had been sitting with other basketball guys—no, thank you—so it's not like I had anybody else to sit with anyway.

"Millie—Amelia, sorry—I doubt I'll 'love' anything in drama class." I spooned dressing onto the side of my sad-looking salad. "It's just not my thing."

Izzy squirted ketchup across her pile of fries in a decorative swoosh. "You know what's not my thing? Salad. I wish it was, but no."

"The school salads are a little pathetic, but they're better than those steamed veggies."

Izzy laughed. "Stars, can you imagine if you didn't eat a veggie with a meal?"

"I like vegetables, thank you very much. And I'm eating chicken strips and French fries too. It's not like it's all health food."

"What's with the 'stars' thing, Izzy?" Millie asked. "Is that from a show?"

She grinned and said, "That's an Izzy original, thank you very much."

Millie—no, Amelia—led the way through the process of scanning our prepaid lunch cards and settling at a small, round lunch table. "Tessa, why don't you think you'll like anything in Drama?" she asked as she popped open her juice. She'd opted for a sandwich and chips, which looked much healthier than either Izzy's or my tray.

"It's just not my thing."

"But maybe it *could* be your thing, and you just don't know it yet."

Why did she seem so personally offended that I didn't enjoy drama?

I smiled as I gathered a bite of salad on my fork before saying, "I think I'm a lost cause, and you should give up on me now."

Amelia tossed her long curls over her shoulders where they wouldn't drag in her food. "Never! I'm determined to make a theater nerd out of you. With a little work—" she made a square with her thumbs and forefingers and framed me with it—"you could have an Audrey Hepburn–type stage presence. Very chic and cool."

Something uncomfortable stirred in my chest. *Is that how I came across to Amelia?* I didn't feel chic or cool. I felt like one giant, tensed muscle that didn't know how to relax.

"Ooh, I love Audrey Hepburn," Izzy gushed as she pushed three French fries into her mouth. "*Funny Face*? *Breakfast at Tiffany's*? She's amazing."

"Right?" Amelia's green eyes sparked at Izzy's enthusiasm. I'd never really taken the time to notice, because usually I just noticed Amelia's bright clothes, larger-than-life personality, and, yeah, her size, but Amelia was really pretty. Her smile was infectious.

As Amelia prattled about a specific scene in *My Fair Lady*, which I could only assume was a musical, I spotted Alex departing the lunch line, a tray in his hand. He looked at me and smiled, and I felt myself sit up straighter. *Should I offer for him to sit in the fourth seat at the table? Would he even want to sit with two girls who were geeking out about old musicals? I wasn't sure I wanted to sit here.*

My heart turned to a hummingbird in my chest as I realized Alex might be heading for our table. A noise squeaked from my throat, loud enough that both Amelia and Izzy looked at me, and then turned to see the cause.

Right then Lauren called out, "Alex! Over here!"

I allowed myself to look just long enough to see that she was already at a table with Michael and Cody, plus other athletes I didn't know. The hummingbird in my chest felt like it had crashed against a window. In my peripheral, I saw Alex adjust his course to sit with his friends. Or maybe he'd been headed toward them the whole time. Probably so. Why would he have sat with us when Michael and Cody were an option?

Izzy turned to me, and the pity on her face made me feel ashamed. "Tessa, why didn't you say something?"

"Like what? He didn't want to sit with us."

Amelia made an over-the-top gasping noise and fanned herself. "Well, I never!" she said in mock outrage.

This was only day two of eating lunch together and already her theatrics exhausted me.

Izzy unscrewed the lid on her soda. "You can't just let Lauren have him."

"I'm not 'letting her' do anything." I stabbed at my salad. "Alex is free to make his own choices. He can sit wherever he wants."

"But what if he doesn't think you're a choice?" Her tone was so soft and caring, I had a weird urge to break into tears right there in the cafeteria. *Wouldn't that be great.*

I shrugged and kept my eyes on my lunch. What I knew, that Izzy didn't, was that Alex *knew* I was a choice. Because last year in a moment of bravery, I'd told him I liked him. And he'd frowned and told me in a gentle voice that he'd asked Leilani to homecoming.

"Okay, clearly I'm behind. Are we talking about that boy?" Thankfully Amelia's volume was lower than I would've expected from her. Having Millie Bryan know something private about me was *not* a very comfortable situation.

"No, we're not. We're changing the subject."

Amelia kept staring at Alex. "I recognize him, but we've never had a class together. What's his name?"

How was my face not literally on fire right now? "Alex. Let's talk about something else."

"He's a major athlete, right?"

"Cross-country and basketball." I shoved a huge bite of chicken strip in my mouth so that I couldn't answer any more questions.

Not that my huge bite could prevent Izzy from talking.

"You should see Alex and Tessa at youth group," Izzy said in a low voice, as if confiding private information to Amelia. "They're so cute."

Amelia took a long drink of her juice. "What's with this other chick, though?"

I forced myself to swallow. "Let's pick a new topic."

"Lauren's in youth group with us. She thinks she has a chance with Alex, but he really only has eyes for Tessa."

Amelia pressed a hand to her heart and said a dramatic "That's the cutest thing I've ever heard."

If only it were actually true.

I covered my burning face with my hands. "You guys. *New* topic." I mentally reached for the first Broadway show name I could think of. "*Cats*. That's a good show, right? Or maybe over-rated? I don't know. What do you guys think?"

Amelia fanned herself as she gasped. "Did you just say *overrated*?"

"She's trying to distract you," Izzy said with an eye roll. "Tessa, is Alex friends with Cody?"

"Yeah, why?"

Izzy shrugged, but even her Mexican roots couldn't hide her blush. "He's my neighbor. He's adorbs."

I flinched. "Ew. I hate that word."

"You hate adorbs?"

"Blech. Yes. Just say the real word."

Izzy's smile turned mischievous. "How about hunky? Can I say Cody is hunky?"

I laughed and covered my ears. "That's way worse. Don't say hunky."

Amelia's gaze flicked between us, and then settled on me. "How can you think *Cats* is overrated?"

Izzy giggled, and then saved me from answering. "Why would we talk about *Cats* when we could talk about *Newsies*? Jack Kelly?" She made a show of fanning herself. "Talk about adorbs. And hunky. He's adorbunky. No!" She grabbed my arm and grinned, pleased with herself before saying, "Hunkdorable."

I groaned.

The two of them began to volley lines from musicals to each other, and I felt relieved to not have to engage in conversation. I wished I could pull my hood over myself and physically retreat into my turtle shell.

Instead, I opened Instagram. The first photo in my feed was Mackenzie's bare feet crossed in front of her. Her toenails glittered gold, and in the distance was a beautiful scene of blue sky and palm trees.

> I'm betting my view at lunch > your view at lunch.

I was typing a message about being jealous and that we should talk soon, when my phone buzzed with a text from Dad.

> Sorry last night didn't go so well. I probably should have expected that. The thing is, I have some stuff I want to talk to you about. Call me when you get a chance.

I snorted. *That* wasn't happening.

I turned my phone over and stabbed at my salad some more.

Amelia stretched her arms into the air and yawned so loudly, you would've thought she was on the stage and that the actor notes said to "overdo it." "I'm sooo tired," she groaned.

I glanced around and found several other students watching Amelia with confused or "what a weirdo" expressions. I flushed, and again longed to pull my hood over my head.

Izzy seemed unruffled. "Why so tired?"

"There's this couple at my church who's getting divorced, and my parents were trying to talk them out of it. They're not counselors or anything, but my dad's an elder and my mom volunteers at, like, a hundred church things. So they were up so late trying to keep them from making such a huge mistake and it kept me up late too."

I felt Izzy look at me, and I tried to keep my face blank and my gaze steady on Amelia.

"How'd it go?" My voice came out flat.

Amelia said with a shrug, "They're still going to get the divorce. I don't know how my parents keep at it, honestly. This is the third couple they've tried to talk sense into, and it never works no matter what they say."

Izzy's gaze skittered between Amelia and me. "Maybe they have a good reason for getting divorced?"

"My parents say there's never a good reason. I know it's not what culture says, but the Bible is pretty clear." Amelia shrugged and continued, "My parents say none of the couples really care about what God wants for them. They're just tired of being married and divorce is the easiest."

I scooted my chair back and grabbed my half-eaten lunch. "I gotta go."

"Tessa . . ." Izzy attempted. I knew she felt bad, but I wasn't about to just sit there and let Amelia talk like her family had it all together unlike those of us with divorcing parents.

From my seat, not every spouse got the choice of divorce, and *easy* was the last adjective I'd use to describe it.

Chapter
9

THE END-OF-CLASS BELL in Algebra II always sparked dread, because that meant it was time for Drama. The only part of class I hadn't minded was when we discussed theater terms like down-stage and cue. Maybe we'd do more vocab today, and it would take up a lot of time. A girl could hope, anyway.

As I headed toward the arts hall, I heard a "Tessa!" behind me.

I turned to see Lauren hustling to catch up with me, her blond ponytail bouncing behind her. She had large, brown eyes like a Disney princess. Or maybe they weren't actually large but only looked that way because she took the time to put on not just mascara, but eyeliner and eyeshadow too. She posted a tutorial on Instagram last night about how to simplify your makeup routine when you only had fifteen minutes. Her simplified routine was more complicated than my regular routine.

"Hey, thanks for waiting," Lauren said, slightly out of breath. "Where you headed?"

"Multipurpose room. Drama."

"Lucky. I have Government." Lauren scrunched her face. "Just three days in and I already think that class is going to be the worst."

"I took that last year. Lots of memorization."

"Yeah." Lauren tucked an imaginary strand of hair behind her ear and sent me a bashful smile. "So, I need to ask you kind of a weird question."

Hopefully it wouldn't take long, since I needed to pee. "Okay."

"Are you and Alex, like, together?"

The air in my lungs pushed out of me in a weird, wheezy laugh. "Alex Hastings? No. We're just friends."

"Okay, that's what I thought. I just . . ." Lauren's giggle sounded nervous. "A friend of mine said she thought she'd heard that you liked him. And since we're sisters in Christ and everything, I just didn't want to . . . you know. Steal your guy or something."

"That's very thoughtful." Which was annoyingly true. "Alex and I are good friends, but he's not my personal property, so it would actually be impossible for you to steal him from me."

"Oh, I didn't mean literally steal, just—"

"I know what you meant." I resisted rolling my eyes. "I was teasing."

"Oh. Okay." Lauren laughed again. "Well, thanks for clarifying. I kinda thought I'd ask him to homecoming. Do you think he'd say yes?"

The hopeful look on her face left me feeling the same way I did when I got kicked in the face by another swimmer. *She was going to ask him to homecoming? Not that it was written down in the school rules anywhere, but boys usually asked girls to homecoming.*

I should be applauding her willingness to push back on tradition, but I was busy trying to not burst into tears in front of her. Somehow, I managed to keep my voice steady and calm. "I don't know, honestly. We don't talk about that kind of stuff."

Except for that one time, of course, when I said, "I really like you, Alex," and he said, "Oh . . . I've asked Leilani to homecoming."

Lauren giggled, which was a super-annoying conversational habit. "I know it's kinda early, but homecoming is really only a few weeks away. And I know at least two other girls who like him. I kinda want to snap him up early, you know?"

Snap him up early. Those had been Mackenzie's exact words to me at the end of eighth grade.

"Sure," I said with a bright smile. "Good luck. I gotta get to class."

"Okay," Lauren chirped. She waved enthusiastically and walked off with even more bounce in her step.

I blew out a long sigh and carried on down the hallway. At least this time I hadn't embarrassed myself by confessing my crush on Alex. If I could handle him liking Leilani, I could handle Lauren asking him to homecoming. I'd hunker down in my turtle shell and be fine.

When I entered the multipurpose room, Amelia was standing at the shoe organizer, typing hastily on her phone. "Hey." She glanced up at me, and then frowned. "You okay?"

No. Not at all.

"Yep." I put on a smile and dropped my phone into the sleeve. "I'm fine."

Her face brightened. "Good."

Maybe I could act after all. I woke up my phone to silence it and saw a new text from Dad. *Ugh. Take a hint!*

"So, I'm super sorry about yesterday at lunch." Amelia put a hand on my arm as I again dropped my phone into the organizer. "I had *no* idea about your parents. Obviously."

I stared at her, and before I knew what was happening, Amelia had wrapped me in one of the most intense hugs I'd ever experienced. My return of the hug felt robotic.

Finally—*finally*—Amelia pulled away but continued to gaze at me with great intensity. "If you want your parents to talk to my parents, just let me know. They would happily do it, even if we're different denominations."

"Uh, okay." I let my hair swing forward, shielding my face. "Thanks."

Izzy had stretched herself across the black-and-white-striped love seat, saving it for us. A flush of anger came over me as she waved. I couldn't believe she'd told Amelia about my parents. I'd told her that in confidence.

I didn't want to sit with the two of them, but I knew absolutely nobody else in this class. Even still, I ignored Izzy patting the spot beside her on the love seat and sat on the floor instead.

"All right, kiddos, we're doing a fun improv activity today!" Ms. Larkin called as she stood from her desk. "Everybody find a partner."

I didn't even look backward at Izzy and Amelia. I stood and crossed the room to a boy I didn't know, but who wasn't moving to join anybody. "Want to be partners?"

His eyes widened. He had a round face, flat like a dinner plate, and shaggy, nut-brown hair. "Uh, okay . . ."

"I'm Tessa."

"Chad."

Was I imagining Izzy watching me? I certainly wasn't going to turn and look.

"I hate this class," I confessed to Chad. "I don't even know what improv is."

Chad smirked, and it looked funny on his boyish face. "If you already hate drama, this probably won't be your favorite thing we do in here. Improvisation is where you have no script. You just make it up as you go along."

I blinked. "You're kidding me. No script?"

Chad seemed amused by whatever horror-struck expression I had on my face. "Sorry, no. I mean yes. I mean, I'm not kidding and yes, no script."

I buried my face in my hands. *God, what were You thinking when You let me be in this class?*

—∽∽—

Mom was quiet as she navigated the tree-lined streets of Grandma and Grandpa's neighborhood. *Was she quiet because she was nervous about seeing Dad's parents? Or just because she was Mom? She was always quiet these days.*

"So you'll pick me up in a little bit?"

Mom startled, as though she'd forgotten I was in the car too. "I have a therapy appointment at four. I can pick you up after that. You'd still have an hour or so to eat dinner and make it to swimming."

"There's no swimming tonight." My voice came out sharper than I meant for it to. "It's Friday."

"Oh." Mom shook her head, as if clearing out something. "Right."

Why did I keep waiting for her to acknowledge that I had made it through the first few days of sophomore year? While we had no official traditions around this, it felt like Normal Mom would have planned something—a movie, a bowl of ice cream— for the first Friday of the school year. Something small, but something, nonetheless.

Dad might be the one who was physically absent, but sometimes Mom felt just as gone.

My phone buzzed. Probably Dad.

Nope, Izzy.

> Hey, is something bothering you? You didn't seem like yourself in Drama, and then you weren't at lunch . . .

I swiped the message away. If she didn't realize what she'd done wrong, I wasn't going to spell it out for her.

Mom pulled up Grandma and Grandpa's steep driveway, put the car in park, and said, "I'll be here around five. If you could just watch for me and come out, that would be great."

So she wasn't coming inside even to say hi. I probably should've seen that coming.

"Okay." I unbuckled and popped open my door. "See you around then."

I navigated the short walkway lined with potted geraniums to the front door of Grandma and Grandpa's ranch house that my dad and aunt had been raised in. Grandma had called me after school asking if I wanted to come over for cookies. I'd almost said no, but that had left me feeling guilty. I hadn't talked to her or Grandpa since Dad dropped the divorce bomb on all of us.

Grandma opened the door before I had the chance to knock and threw her arms around me. Thanks to Amelia, it was only the second-most-intense hug I'd had that day.

"How are you, honey?" Her watery voice suggested she was not okay.

"I'm fine," I said into her shoulder.

Grandma held me at arm's length, and then frowned behind me. "Your mother isn't coming in?"

I looked over my shoulder, catching the bumper of Mom's SUV before it pulled out of sight. "She was running late for an appointment."

Grandma continued frowning at the space where Mom's Lexus had been. "I certainly hope she doesn't plan to just pull in the driveway and honk when she comes to pick you up. I'd like to think we can all be adults here."

Was my mom not acting like an adult? She seemed like a sad adult, certainly, but she'd brought me with no complaints, hadn't she?

Grandma offered a reassuring smile as she guided me through the doorway. "Not for you to worry about, Tessa. None of us have ever been in this situation before, and we're all bound to fumble a bit. We'll need grace in abundance. Tell me, how have the first few days of school been?"

I slipped off my flip-flops. "Tiring."

"Cookies will help. Do you want tea with them?"

Even when it was ninety degrees outside, Grandma drank hot tea in the afternoon. "Sure."

"Good. I already started the water." Grandma headed for the kitchen, and I followed. "Grandpa had to run to the hardware store because that bathroom faucet is leaking again, but he should be back soon."

"Okay." I took a seat at the counter, the way I had all my life. The way my dad and aunt probably had all their lives too. "How has your day been?"

Grandma released a slow sigh. "I'm not even sure how to answer that question, honey. Ever since we had lunch with your father and he told us about—" Grandma fluttered her hand, as if that was enough to indicate the impending divorce—"I just can't seem to do anything but eat and cry, with a little bit of prayer thrown in there."

Grandma looked at me, and all her heartache was on display in her eyes. She still did a full face of makeup most days, but she hadn't bothered with eye makeup this afternoon. Or maybe she'd already cried it off.

The glimpse of Grandma's raw emotion had me longing to retreat into my shell. I looked away from her sadness. "Yeah, I know what you mean."

Grandma nudged a platter of carmelitas at me. "The man I had lunch with sure looked like my David. His voice sounded like my David. But the words he was saying just made no sense to me—that Rebecca is a gift from God for him. That God wants us to be able to correct youthful mistakes, not live in them our entire lives. All kinds of hooey like that."

Rebecca was a gift from God, but marrying my mother—the

relationship that resulted in me—was a youthful mistake? The words felt like knives. I struggled to keep my face calm. "What did you say to that?"

"That he was wasting his breath if he was trying to convince me that God wanted him to divorce his wife and abandon his child. That he was being selfish and trying to use God as justification." Grandma poured hot water into my cup, and I watched as the water morphed into English breakfast tea. "He has blinders on, that's all there is to it. He's going to wake up one day and realize he walked away from a perfectly fine life."

The phrase *perfectly fine* sounded like an insult to my ears. Nobody longed for a "perfectly fine" life. You wanted a good life. A great life. A "life worth sharing," as Rebecca would say.

Maybe it was stupid, but I wanted Grandma to revise her comment. I wanted her to acknowledge that our life had been perfect, but then Dad screwed it up.

Instead, Grandma plopped the teakettle back on the stovetop with more force than necessary. "I said to him, 'David, how's Carrie going to support herself? Much less Tessa. Carrie's just an artist. She probably can't afford groceries on her own, let alone that huge house and fancy SUV.' He says he'll take care of it, but I really don't understand how he plans to support you *and* your mother *and* this new woman."

"Mom makes money." I wasn't totally sure of this, but I wanted it to be true. "Her art classes are almost all at capacity."

Which made me realize, I hadn't seen any evidence that she was planning to teach her fall art classes. Usually as soon as I was back in school, she was getting supplies in order to start strong the day after Labor Day.

"I'm not saying she isn't talented, Tessa. I'm saying your mom hasn't had to make her own way in the world for quite some time. I warned her about that when she quit work to have you—that life is more curveballs than anything else—but even I couldn't have predicted this."

I loved my grandma, but her suggestion that my mom shouldn't have stayed home with me had that creature behind my rib cage feeling itchy with anger. I stared into the safety of my tea, waiting for the emotion to clear from my face.

"Please don't worry, Tessa." Grandma reached across the counter and cupped my arm. "Grandpa and I would always take care of you."

I tried to smile. "I know."

But what about Mom? Would they take care of her, too, or would they ultimately side with Dad if they had to? He was their son, after all.

Grandma squeezed my arm and released. "Hopefully your father comes to his senses soon and comes home."

I huffed a humorless laugh. "I have a hard time imagining that happening."

"Oh, God can work all kinds of miracles. Grandpa and I have known loads of couples whose marriages survived worse. If two people decide to work it out, there's not much that can stop them." Grandma sighed. "We just need your father to make the decision."

Everyone acted like Dad was in charge of deciding if he and Mom reconciled. Like if Dad decided to walk away from his life of sin and rejoin the marriage, that would be that.

"The good news is, your dad seemed as committed as ever to your trip to Iceland. I was relieved to hear that!"

"He's capable of keeping some promises, I guess." As deserved as I felt the words were, guilt sloshed in my stomach.

How badly did Dad want to go to Iceland? What would he do, I wondered, if I gave him an ultimatum? I'll still go to Iceland, but only if you're in marriage counseling with Mom. That was worth a shot, right?

My phone buzzed again, and I glanced at it. Izzy.

I'm sorry if what Amelia said about divorce hurt your feelings. I told her about your parents, so she won't do that again.

I rolled my eyes at the screen before typing my reply.

That was private information I trusted you with. You shouldn't have told her.

Grandma took another cookie from the plate. "He says you haven't really talked to him since he left. I said, 'David, can you blame the girl?' But Tessa, honey, you really should talk to your dad. I know you're angry, but there are two sides to every story."

I blinked a few times. My phone buzzed, but I ignored it. "He cheated on my mom and is living with another woman. What other side of that story do I need to know?"

Grandma flinched. "Yes, I know. And of course, it's horrible and a sin and all those things. I'm not excusing his poor behavior. But a man doesn't wander if . . ."

The unsaid words dangled between us, and my heart squeezed in my chest. My phone buzzed two more times as I stared at Grandma.

The garage door went up, signaling Grandpa's return, and Grandma looked relieved by the interruption. As she scurried out to the garage with claims of needing to help him in with the bags, my phone buzzed again. All four messages were from Izzy.

Tessa! I'm so sorry! I didn't even think about that.
I won't tell anybody else, and I'll tell Amelia it's private, so she doesn't tell anyone else.
I'm so sorry. Please forgive me. I'll never do that again!

And then a full row of weeping emojis.

I took a deep breath. She was asking for forgiveness, and the right thing to do was forgive her, even if I didn't feel like it. Fake it until you make it, as the saying went.

I forgive you, I typed. Then I scrolled back to our texts the night I told her. I didn't tell you it was private.

I mean, she should've realized, but still. I set my phone aside and shoved a whole carmelita in my mouth. When my phone buzzed again, I laughed out loud. Izzy, predictably, had texted, I still feel terrible. What kind of cupcakes can I make you???

Chapter
10

As I WALKED INTO Grounds and Rounds Coffee Shop, April and Leilani came out.

"Hi!" April cried out, giving me a hug that involved very little touching. Like the opposite of an Amelia hug. "What are you up to?"

Each of them held a variety of iced coffee in one hand and shopping bags in the other. I felt a prick of hurt feelings that I hadn't been invited.

"Just . . . meeting my dad for coffee." I tried to smile and maybe got 50% of the way there.

Both April and Leilani put on somber masks. "Yeah, we saw him inside," Leilani said. "I wish we actually had classes together at school. I never see you anymore."

"Yeah, I know. My schedule is ridiculous. They were supposed to put me in Organic Farming, and instead I'm in Drama."

April made a face. "Is that why I've seen you a couple of times with Millie Bryan?"

"Amelia," I corrected without thinking about it. "Yeah."

"She's a weirdo. All theater people are *so* bizarre." April cocked her hip and took a long drink from her straw.

Should I say something kind about Amelia? Of course, it's not like April was completely wrong. Amelia was kinda weird . . .

Leilani rattled the ice in her cup. "Who's Amelia?"

"You'd recognize her if you saw her. She's that really fat girl always wearing clothes she shouldn't. Red hair, super loud." April smoothed her own dress, as if to reassure herself of her own size and style.

If they'd been looking at me, they would've seen me flinch. So, yes, Amelia was bigger. But *fat* didn't seem like the right word choice. *And clothes she shouldn't wear? What did that even mean? It's not like Amelia wore anything revealing.*

"Oh, yeah." Leilani crinkled her nose like she'd smelled something gross. "With the really big red hair? I think we have Spanish together. She'll do anything for attention. Which I really don't get. If I was her size, I'd be embarrassed to leave the house!"

April and Leilani both laughed, and not only did my stomach ache with guilt, but my whole body felt flushed with anger at hearing Amelia talked about like that.

"She's a really nice person . . ." I hated how weak my voice sounded. I swallowed and tried to gather my thoughts. *Should I say she couldn't help how big she was? I'd never seen her parents. Maybe Amelia being overweight was genetic. Or should I say—*

"I'm sure she is," Leilani said flippantly. "If you hate it so much, why don't you drop the class?"

This was a better line of conversation. If the topic steered away from Amelia, I wouldn't have to defend her. "I need my fine-arts credit. I'm just trying to buck up and get through it, but it's the worst."

Leilani trapped her black hair with her free hand as it blew in the breeze. "Want to come out with us tonight? We're getting together with Noah and his friends."

April elbowed her. "Noah said there'd be a keg. Good Girl Tessa won't come if there's drinking." April winked at me, like she was teasing. She was right, but it still felt like one more brick in the wall that divided me from them. A wall that had been growing since we started high school.

"Oh, right." Leilani shrugged at me and said, "You don't have to drink. You can just come hang out."

"Thanks, but no thanks," I said with another one of my attempted smiles.

Leilani rolled her eyes. "You know who is basically your soulmate? Alex. I swear *fun* is a dirty word to him."

I huffed an awkward laugh and glanced at April. I knew Leilani had been told about my crush on Alex. She'd apparently never seen me as a threat to her, because the information had just slipped right out of that brain of hers. Or at least that's what I assumed from her utter lack of sensitivity around me.

April's laugh rang a bit high and false. "Well, if you change your mind, let us know. Enjoy your coffee!"

And then she pulled Leilani away, presumably off for more shopping. Regret pinged in my heart. I used to really enjoy shopping with April. I wished we were still close like in middle school.

I turned my back to their retreating figures and pulled open the door to Grounds and Rounds. Normally, I would engage my senses to savor entering my favorite coffeehouse. I would breathe deeply the scent of coffee beans and cinnamon. I would perk my ears for whatever they had playing on the sound system. My mouth would be salivating with the thought of my hazelnut latte.

But today, all those sensory details I typically loved about Grounds and Rounds faded to the background as I scanned the faces of other patrons. Dad waved to me from a booth in the back. He had his laptop out and a stack of papers beside him that looked like work. I waved back—*did I always wave so jerkily?*—and motioned that I was going to order. He stood and reached for the wallet in his back pocket. I held up a gift card I'd won in a youth group raffle over the summer. Dad sat back down. I wished there was a line at the register so I could put off this conversation a bit longer, but instead I ordered, paid, and was promised my latte would be right out all within a minute.

During that time, Dad had put away his work. His smile looked forced as I approached. "Hi."

"Hi."

I scooted into the booth on the other side from him and arranged my handbag just so.

"Did you see April and Leilani?" he asked.

"I did."

"They looked like they were having fun."

I nodded as I stared at the scarred wooden table. At least my nervousness about talking to Dad had eclipsed my hurt feelings of April and Leilani not including me in their shopping plans. A tarnished silver lining in a very dark cloud.

The cheerful employee who'd taken my order placed my latte on the table. "Here you are, Tessa. Enjoy!"

"Thanks."

Dad watched him walk away. "You know him?"

I turned my cup so he could see my name scribbled in black Sharpie. "Nope."

He smiled and said, "Ah. I'm going to run to the restroom real quick. I worried if I went before you arrived, I would lose our table. It's busy this morning."

I popped the lid off my coffee. "Yeah."

"Be right back." Dad strode down the back hall to where the bathrooms were tucked away.

I cupped my hands around the paper cup and inhaled the

hazelnut scent. I could do this. I would just say it plainly: *"Dad, I asked you to meet me so we could talk about our Iceland trip. If you would like for us to go, then I need you to commit to starting marriage counseling with Mom."*

I took my phone out of my purse so I'd have something to do besides stress and repeat the minuscule script I'd written for myself. On Instagram, I was greeted by a picture of Alex's new running shoes. I smiled. He was so nerdy about running, and I found it utterly charming.

Next was a picture of Mackenzie and her cousin doing yoga poses on the beach. I frowned. *When was the last time I had talked to Mackenzie?* Our texting had tapered off since school started, and I'd had to cancel our last two phone calls because of swimming and homework. *I should really call her today. Not that it looked like she was missing me much with her fab beach lifestyle.*

I picked up my latte and took a sip. Out of habit, I pulled up Rebecca's profile to see what new cutesy printable or classroom idea she had for me today.

The new post loaded.

My cup slipped from my hand and splattered latte all over my lap. I let out a loud curse as the heat stung on my skin.

My dad, who had been returning from the bathroom, came jogging back. "Oh no, Tessa."

"I'll make you a new one," promised the same employee as he jogged over with a roll of paper towels, a long tail of them trailing behind.

My face burned as I ignored the mess and glared at my dad. I shoved my phone in his face. "When were you going to tell me that Rebecca's pregnant?"

Chapter
11

THE COFFEE SHOP EMPLOYEE froze mid-swipe of the table.

"I was going to tell you today, honey." Dad had his hands up in front of him, like a man showing the police he was unarmed. But these days, it felt like he was the weapon. "I promise. I didn't know . . ." He gestured to my phone. "I didn't realize you followed Rebecca, or I would've asked her to wait another day."

"I'm just gonna go get you a new latte," the employee mumbled as he scurried away, leaving the paper towels.

Thick sarcasm boiled out of me. "Not announce this glorious news on Instagram *today*? What a huge disappointment that would be to all her followers." I scrolled the comments with a vicious swipe. "I mean, Luv2teach said this post made her whole week. And Librarian Janna is so happy for you guys. These are definitely the people who need to be prioritized when deciding how to announce a pregnancy."

Dad looked frantically around the coffeehouse, and I realized just how quiet our surrounds had become and just how loud I'd been talking. He dropped his voice low. "Tessa, you're making a scene—"

"What did you think was going to happen when you told me in a public place, Dad?" I threw my phone into my purse. "Did you think I was going to volunteer to throw you a baby shower? Maybe host a gender-reveal party?"

A woman in her twenties with dusky skin and wideset dark eyes approached the table. From her professional smile, I could tell she was the manager even before she opened her mouth.

"Hey, guys, I need you to either lower your volume or take this conversation outside—"

"I'm very sorry." The first blush of shame came over me. "Let me just finish cleaning this up, and I'll go."

"We can take care of it, miss. And Wilson already has a new drink for you at the counter." The manager gestured to the coffee bar, where the employee held up a new latte, giving me a tentative smile along with it.

I glanced around Grounds and Rounds and found everyone very pointedly *not* looking at me, with the exception of a few children who stared openly.

"Sorry, everyone," I surprised myself by saying. I wanted to justify myself, wanted to say, *If you just found out on Insta that your dad's girlfriend is pregnant, you'd react the same way.* Instead I just said to the manager, "I'm really, really sorry," and grabbed my purse.

"So sorry about the mess," I said to the employee as he held out my latte.

He offered me a sympathetic smile. "Don't worry about it."

Outside, as I charged down the sidewalk in the sticky August air, Dad followed close behind. "We need to talk about this, Tessa."

"Okay. Should I just leave my comment on Rebecca's announcement? Or maybe DM—"

"Enough with the cute comments—"

I whirled on the sidewalk, stepping out of my flip-flop in the process. "And enough with you critiquing how I'm responding. Guess what, Dad? That's one thing you don't get to choose. You don't get to choose how I feel, or what I say, or how loudly I say it. You also don't get to choose if I get on that plane to Iceland in October, and hell would have to freeze over before I did."

Dad looked like I'd slapped him, and I didn't care. I even *liked* that he looked hurt.

"Do you realize that in all of this, you've never once said *sorry* to me?" I laughed, but it sounded more like a hysterical sob. Maybe it was. I tried sliding my foot back in my flip-flop, but I couldn't seem to get it in. "You've never even asked me to forgive you. You just want me to—" my hands flailed as I searched for words, and for the second time that morning, hot coffee sloshed onto my skin—"condone what you've done or give you my blessing or something. And I'm telling you right now, that's never going to happen. I'm never going to accept you and Rebecca, and even if you beg me the rest of your life, I'm never forgiving you for what you did to our family."

My stupid foot still wouldn't go into my stupid shoe, so I just picked it up and marched away, but this time, Dad didn't follow. With everything that had happened, I wouldn't have expected his passivity to hurt in that moment, but him letting me walk away still pierced.

—⁓—

". . . So Mom was like, 'Why did you even leave the stuffed dragon on your desk? You know what Sebastian is like,'" Izzy chattered as we navigated the hallways to the multipurpose room. "Which is so typical. Not only am I basically trapped in the house watching my little brother on a holiday weekend, but now it's my fault that he stole my dragon off my desk, because I left it out!"

I'd met Izzy's younger brother at church a couple of times. He was in sixth grade and the first person I'd ever interacted with who was on the autism spectrum. Every conversation I'd attempted with him felt awkward, but Izzy said he really liked me.

I tried to infuse feeling into my voice. "That's rough. I'm so sorry."

Izzy didn't seem to mind or notice how flat my words sounded. "It'll be fine. Though one of these days, I'm also going to get a job, just like my sister, Claire, and Mom and Dad will have to find somebody else to watch him." She blew out a blustery sigh. "Enough of that. How was your Labor Day weekend? Oh! I've wanted to ask you, but it never seems like the right time. How are things with your parents?"

I swallowed hard as a rush of anger and sadness surged, pushing them back down inside my shell. "Uh, same. Fine."

"Fine?"

I hesitated and Izzy noticed. "You don't have to answer if you don't want to."

We had maybe a minute before we reached Drama. How, exactly, would I summarize?

After the humiliating scene at Grounds and Rounds, I walked all the way home because I didn't want to call my mom and ask her to pick me up. I didn't want to tell her about the baby over the phone. But when I arrived nearly an hour later, Dad had already called her and told her the news.

So, on a weekend that my mom normally spent happily piddling around in the basement studio getting ready for students, she instead barely moved off the couch, barely talked, and only ate when I brought her food. She really only cried at night. Maybe when she thought I was sleeping and wouldn't hear.

Meanwhile, on Instagram, I learned Rebecca and Dad had driven to Chicago at some point after my botched coffee date. She'd posted multiple photo series, plus several stories about seeing a game at Wrigley Field—"*something my man has always wanted to do!*"—and doing all the other Chicago things. I'd searched my dad's face in the pictures for hints that he was upset, not sleeping well, or that I'd somehow wounded him.

Instead, he looked like he was living his best life.

"It's not that I don't want to talk about it," I said to Izzy as we sidestepped a group of senior girls heading into the bathroom. "But now doesn't seem great."

"You're handling this whole thing so well. If *my* parents were divorcing, I would be an absolute mess."

I am *an absolute mess*, the words sat on my tongue, tasting sharp and bitter.

Inside the multipurpose room, we dropped our phones into the shoe organizer and headed toward what had become our usual grouping of seats. Amelia was already on the love seat, chatting away with a girl I didn't recognize. When Amelia spotted us, she threw her hand in the air and gave such an exuberant wave that several students turned to look at us, including the girl she'd been talking to.

The girl had slouched shoulders, a low, honey-colored ponytail, and well-worn cowboy boots that looked too functional to be a fashion choice. She scanned Izzy and me, seeming wary.

"Girls, this is Shay Mitchell," Amelia said as we approached. "She's new. Not just to Drama, but to Northside. Shay, this is Izzy and Tessa. Izzy is new this year too, but Tessa and I both grew up in Riverbend."

Shay's smile showed only a glimpse of her teeth. She offered a small wave. "Nice to meet you."

Even though her voice sounded clear and strong, Shay didn't seem particularly comfortable. She glanced around the multipurpose room like one might a haunted house.

I nudged the red beanbag chair closer to the love seat before I planted myself in it. "You too."

Izzy plopped into the rocking chair on the other side of Shay. "Where'd you move from?"

Shay hesitated, as though it was a tough question to answer. "Buck Creek."

"Oh!" Izzy brightened. "By Lafayette? I just moved from Williamsport. Ever heard of it?"

Shay shook her head.

"It's teeny tiny, but I bet it's only an hour or so from Buck Creek. When we moved, I was really hoping for somewhere big like Indianapolis. Or Boston. Or New York City." Izzy gave a dramatic sigh. "But alas. Riverbend."

"NYC is the absolute best." Amelia's voice inched up in volume. "I've never been, but I'm just dying to go. I *have* to live there when I'm a grown-up. Oh, here's Ms. Larkin!"

Amelia jumped to her feet and waved with the urgency of a first grader who'd just realized she had to pee *right now*. "Ms. Larkin! We have a new student!"

Shay's gaze darted around the room, and she sunk back into the corner of the love seat. *How had she wound up in Intro to Drama?*

"Thank you, Amelia." Ms. Larkin's voice had a calm pitch to it, as if she sensed that Shay didn't love the spotlight. Not that it took much intuition. She offered Shay a hand and a kind smile. "You must be Shay. It's nice to meet you."

Shay stood and shook Ms. Larkin's hand and offered a shy smile. "You too."

"I'm glad to have you in my class."

Shay huffed a quiet laugh and folded her arms around herself. "I've never been in any kind of class like this."

Could Ms. Larkin hear the same subtext that I could? I don't want to be here either.

"I promise you that's true of at least half the kiddos in here, Shay. I will ask you to stretch your comfort zone, but I won't grade you on if you're the next Meryl Streep or not. Sound fair?"

Shay nodded but didn't look any more relaxed.

"This is actually a great first day for you to be here, because we're starting one-act plays. I'll just add you to Amelia's group, since you already know each other." Ms. Larkin tapped away with her stylus on her iPad. Then she smiled at Izzy and me before saying, "Izzy and Tessa are your other group members, so your seating arrangement is perfect."

Amelia raised her hand as she asked, "What play are we doing?"

"I'll get class started, and then we'll talk in more detail, okay?"

Ms. Larkin strolled to the center of the rug, her long skirt swishing, and Shay retook her spot on the love seat.

Amelia beamed at all of us. "One Acts are the best. You guys are going to love this."

"I knew you were going to say that." To Shay, I added, "Everything with Amelia is either the best or the worst. Very little room for anything in between."

Shay gave me a mild smile as she pressed herself back into the love seat, like she hoped it would open up and swallow her.

Amelia laughed. "Tessa, I'm serious. I think you'll love doing a One Act. I'm just glad I get to participate, even though I'm not technically taking this class. I'm a TA."

Like we didn't all know. I was betting even Shay had been told multiple times.

"I'm excited." Izzy rubbed her hands together. "I've never done a One Act."

"I don't mean to sound stupid," Shay edged into the conversation. "But what's a One Act?"

So she was a little awkward, but I had a feeling I would get along just fine with this girl.

Chapter

12

A MESSAGE CAME INTO the Snapchat group Amelia had created for Izzy, Shay, and me at lunch. She'd set this up as if it were the most obvious next right step.

"Now that we're doing the One Act together," she'd said, "we'll need to be in contact all the time. Shay, what's your username on Snap?"

Shay blinked rapidly, as if processing the odd turn in events. She had eyes the color of a latte, framed by thick, brown lashes that I was guessing had never known a mascara wand. "Um, I don't have one."

Amelia raised her eyebrows. "Strict parents?"

Shay visibly swallowed and ducked her head. "No. I guess I could get one . . ."

"Yep. Let's do it now. Are you on school Wi-Fi?"

As Amelia snatched up Shay's phone, I wanted to apologize

to her—*Sorry Amelia is being so aggressive*—but didn't know how without hurting Amelia's feelings. While Shay was polite, she didn't seem overeager to become besties with us and probably didn't realize accepting the invitation to sit at our lunch table would lead to Amelia taking her phone, downloading an app, and being verbally prompted through setting up a Snapchat account.

I probably would've spoken up more, but I was preoccupied with sulking into my lunch tray. The One Acts were being performed Saturday, October 5, just a few days after my sixteenth birthday. The day I was supposed to fly to Reykjavík. If my dad wasn't having a midlife crisis and I was still going to Iceland, I wouldn't have had to do this stupid play.

"Okay." Amelia tapped away at her phone. "You'll all be getting invitations. We're going to be spending a lot of time together outside of school. We probably don't need to rehearse *every* day, but I think at least three days. Maybe four. Izzy, what days work best for you?"

"Whoa, whoa, whoa," I jumped in. "I already have swim practice four nights a week."

Amelia made a sound like a growl in her throat. "Okay, fine. What time is swimming?"

"Seven to eight."

"Oh, okay. So, plenty of time after school, then."

"I can't after school," Izzy said with a sigh. "I have to babysit my brother after school."

Amelia looked impatient. "*Every* day, though? Can't you tell your parents it's for a school assignment? I'm sure they'd understand."

I held up my hand in a stop-right-there kind of gesture. "This is a school assignment of a twenty-minute show, and it's a month away. We'll have class time, so—"

"That's not going to be enough. Not for a quality production."

Shay nibbled at her peanut butter sandwich, looking like she wished she could just scoot her chair away and join another group.

"Amelia, *I'm* in this production," I said, "so we already know it's not going to be the kind of quality you want—"

"If you would just relax onstage—"

"On top of that—" sometimes you just had to talk louder than Amelia if you wanted to be heard—"I still need time for homework and dinner. I cannot give every moment after school to a dumb one-act play for the next month. And Izzy has responsibilities at home."

Izzy popped open her applesauce container. "Maybe we don't need to make a decision right now. Maybe we can see how much we get done in class, and then in a week revisit if we need some after-school rehearsals?"

"Sounds good." I clipped off the last of Izzy's sentence in an effort to beat Amelia's rejection of the idea. "Shay? Could you do that?"

Shay shrugged and said, "Sure."

Amelia let out a gusty sigh with an added "Fine," and had let the subject drop.

Now that I was at swim practice, my phone buzzed insistently. Amelia was sending set ideas for our play, *Snowfall in October*, and the text was all exclamation points and heart emojis. I zipped my phone into its waterproof pocket. I could think about that later.

As I stripped off my sweatshirt, I glanced at the pool, where the younger swimmers who practiced in the time slot before us waited in bobbing lines to do flip turns. Kayleigh chatted with another girl, looking happy and normal. I waved to her, but she didn't see me.

"Hey, Tessa." Abraham plopped his swim bag onto the bench next to mine. "I think I parked next to you in the lot. You drive a Honda Civic, right?"

"I don't have a car. I walk here."

"Oh, funny. I thought I saw you in a black Honda Civic once."

I dug past my flippers and kickboard for my cap and goggles, which always got buried on the bottom. "My friend drives a Honda Civic. Maybe it was his."

"That guy who was at the preseason meet?"

I twisted my ponytail into a bun and secured it with an elastic. "Yep."

Did Alex know Rebecca was pregnant? Had my mom told his mom? Probably not, or I would've heard from him. I needed to text Mackenzie and tell her, but telling people felt complicated. Made the pregnancy feel real.

Coach Shauna barked a correction at one of the boys, and I glanced toward the pool. This time Kayleigh waved at me, and I waved back.

"I bet you never get yelled at like that." Abraham's eyes shone with something I couldn't quite identify. *Mischief? Flirtation?*

I frowned and felt my neck go hot. I didn't want any of the other girls thinking I was stupid enough to flirt with Abraham. "Not for goofing off, but plenty of times for doing stuff wrong."

"Really? I've never seen you make a single mistake."

I felt flattered and uncomfortable all at once. "That's just because you haven't hung out with me long enough."

"You know what the other guys call you?"

Now my discomfort ratcheted up. "I don't think I want to know."

"The Perfect Girl. When Coach Shauna sent me to find you at the meet that day, I asked the guys who you were. They told me, 'She's that perfect girl,' and I knew exactly who they meant."

I couldn't even look at Abraham now. I bent at the waist and stretched my swim cap over my knot of hair. How could you feel pleased and vulnerable all at once? *Was I so transparent that a serial flirter like Abraham could easily see what would flatter me most?*

"Did I embarrass you?" Abraham sounded more amused than apologetic. "Let's talk about me instead. What do the girls say about me?"

I straightened and began tucking stray strands of hair into my cap. "Nothing."

A complete lie, but Abraham's ego hardly needed feeding.

Instead of looking dejected, Abraham brightened. "Guess what?" He reached into his swim bag and pulled out a silver swim cap that matched mine. "We're swim-cap buddies. Same brand and everything."

"Adorable," I said flatly as I folded my extra clothes and placed them in my bag.

"We're going to need a picture of us." Abraham tugged on his cap with enviable ease. "C'mon."

I rolled my eyes. "We don't need a picture."

"Yes, we do." Abraham opened the camera app on his phone. "Though I'll warn you, I'm using you. I want to post it on Instagram and make all my friends at Providence Day jealous that I know such a pretty girl."

Heat bloomed in my cheeks, and I felt a stab of annoyance with myself. *How could I allow myself to feel flattered?* Yesterday I'd seen him flirt with Jace before practice, Lindsey during, and Lexi afterward. I was way too smart for this.

Still, I couldn't quite ignore the pleasure that filled my chest from being called pretty by a cute boy my own age. And his comment gave me an idea. What if I posted the picture on my Instagram too? Maybe it wasn't #YOLO worthy, but unless my dad had completely changed in all his principles, it could really freak him out. He had always told me I was too young to date anybody—yet another reason why I'd never tried to "snatch up" Alex—so if I worded the post right, I could really get under Dad's skin.

I leaned closer to Abraham and dragged out my biggest, happiest smile. He snapped the selfie and then pulled off his cap. "I'll text it to you so you can make that guy jealous if you want. What's your number?"

As I gave him my number, Coach Shauna blew her whistle for the young kids to get out of the pool, and I laid my towel neatly beside my swim bag. Abraham watched; his eyebrows hoisted.

"What?"

"I'm watching you live up to your nickname, that's all."

I rolled my eyes, grabbed my goggles, and walked away. *Stop feeling so special*, I told myself. He was just going to turn his attention to one of the other girls now. I'd been watching this play out for weeks.

But when Coach Shauna assigned us to the same lane, Abraham made a show of racing me or egging me on, and I found myself enjoying the lighthearted fun of competing and teasing with him.

As I walked home, I got the notification that @therealabraham had tagged me in a picture. After weeks of following him on Instagram, it felt a little strange to see a picture of myself on his feed alongside pictures of him waterskiing at the lake over the weekend and doing cool stuff with pretty people I didn't know. Seeing me in that context was like seeing a version of myself that I liked better. Someone who maybe could be that pretty, perfect girl Abraham had claimed I was. Someone who was living her best, most share-worthy life.

With my heart pounding, I opened the picture Abraham had texted me. Looking at me like that, pressed close to a boy who wasn't wearing a shirt, I just knew my dad was going to freak. I tweaked the filter—lighting in the aquatic center was always so garish—and typed a caption: Swim cap twinning with @therealabraham at #BlazersIN tonight. I considered saying something more suggestive about our relationship, but while I wouldn't mind my dad getting the wrong idea, I didn't want Abraham to. I added a heart emoji. Then deleted it. Then added it again. So what if Abraham thought I was flirting back? I knew I wasn't.

For just a second, my thumb hesitated over the word *Post*, and then I made public the captured moment.

"Hey, Tessa."

I startled at the sound of Clark Hastings' voice, and found him dribbling the basketball in what appeared to be a game of one-on-one with Alex in their driveway. Both of them had sweat-soaked hair sticking to their foreheads. "Oh, hey."

"You shouldn't walk while you look at your phone, you know." Clark dribbled the ball in a circle around himself. "Haven't seen you in a while. On your way home from swimming?"

"Yep." I hitched my bag higher as I paused at the end of their driveway. "How are you?"

Clark said with a shrug, "No complaints."

Alex wiped his forehead with his sleeve. "Were you walking that trail by yourself again?"

"Maybe."

Alex frowned. "Isn't it kinda dark for that?"

Before I could answer, Clark passed the ball to Alex and jogged off into the garage to pick up his ringing phone. Alex watched, then turned to me, rolled his eyes, and wagged his head. "Teens and their phones these days."

I grinned and said, "Clark has always been highly distractible."

"He gets serious FOMO." Alex smoothed his hair back and it stuck straight up. "Sometimes I text him just to watch him jump to grab his phone. It's like a sickness."

"You torturing your brother is like a sickness? Or his fear of missing out?"

"Probably both."

We smiled at each other, and as the conversation lulled, I realized I should get home. As I opened my mouth to say I would see him in class tomorrow, Alex shifted.

"I have something to talk to you about. I was gonna call you, but . . ." He swallowed, broadcasting his nervousness, and my heart immediately set off racing. *Was he going to ask me to homecoming? This isn't exactly how I hoped this would go—me smelling of* chlorine, him sweaty from basketball, and Clark twenty feet away, but that was fine.

I tucked my bangs behind my ears and said what I hoped sounded like a casual "What's up?"

"You know Lauren?"

Oh. That's where this was going.

"Yeah, of course. She's so nice." The pitch of my voice sounded like I was leading a pep rally. Gooooo, Lauren!

"Yeah, she's nice. She actually . . ." Alex dribbled the basketball, and I felt jealous that he had something for his hands to do while mine hung awkwardly at my sides. "This is kinda weird, but she asked me to go to homecoming with her . . ."

Alex trailed off as if he wasn't sure that should be the end of his sentence. He looked at me through his eyelashes, gauging my reaction. *Trying to figure out how hurt I was? After last year, he obviously knew that I'd want him to ask me.*

I mentally pulled up my protective turtle shell and pushed my smile higher. "Yeah, Lauren actually mentioned a couple of weeks ago that she was planning to ask you. I'm a little surprised she waited this long."

Laugh, I told myself.

I wheezed.

Okay, don't do that again.

Alex frowned and captured the ball between his arm and waist. "So . . . Lauren mentioned this to you?"

"Yeah."

"And what did you say?"

"That I thought it was a great idea. You guys would be really cute together." I fiddled with my ponytail. "I wish I could be there to actually see you guys, but I'll have to settle for pictures. I have a big swim meet in Indianapolis that weekend."

Alex opened his mouth but didn't speak right away. Probably because I'd veered the conversation into such an awkward me-focused direction. He looked at the ground as he said, "I guess I didn't realize you and Lauren are friends."

"Oh. I don't know that we are. I mean, we're not *not* friends, if you know what I mean." I laughed a wheezy laugh again. "She knows you and I are friends, and she wanted to see if I thought you'd say yes."

"So she asked you if she should ask me," Alex said slowly, and lifted his gaze to meet mine. "And you told her yes."

He had really beautiful eyes. It would be so great if he liked me the way I liked him.

"I did. She really likes you." I gestured up the street, toward my house. "I better go. My mom is having a hard time."

Alex frowned. "Like she's sick or something else?"

I hesitated. "Heartsick."

He resumed dribbling the ball. "Stuff with your dad isn't any better?"

"It's too much to go into now." My swim bag strap cut into my arm and I switched shoulders. "I'll have to fill you in later."

"You know, you can call me anytime," Alex said as I took a step away. "I know you've got Mackenzie or whatever, but . . ."

"Thanks," I said with an attempt of a smile. "See you tomorrow."

I could hear his basketball all the way home. The landscape lights flicked on as I approached, but the windows of the house were dark. My throat cinched shut as I thought about all the other times I'd walked home from swim practice to lit windows and Ella Fitzgerald or the Rolling Stones playing inside. Now the house looked on the outside how it felt on the inside—dead.

The only light in the house was the TV, casting a changing array of blue and white across the dark living room, where Mom stretched across the couch. She lay on her side, a pillow tucked beneath her and her face slack with sleep.

I studied her for a moment, grateful that she had a break from being sad, and then went around the first floor and closed all the blinds. As I moved about the dark house and shut out the outside world, everything I'd stuffed into my turtle shell today began to well up. *Why should Mom be falling asleep alone on the couch while Dad would fall asleep with another woman? Why did my closest friend have to move away just when I needed her most? And why didn't Mackenzie care enough to check in on me? Why did my special trip that I'd been looking forward to for years get stripped away from me and replaced by the worst kind of school assignment? Why did Abraham flirt with me and call me pretty, but Alex just thought of me as his friend?*

I turned off the TV and trudged upstairs. I knew I should shower, should at least rinse the chlorine from my hair, but even the idea of showering felt overwhelming.

At youth group and on Sunday mornings, the adults always talked about God being close to us in our hard times, but He sure didn't feel close. I must be doing something wrong. Not reading my Bible enough, serving enough, praying enough.

That's what I should do. I should pray. Maybe then God wouldn't feel so removed from everything hard in my life.

I sunk onto my bed. "Dear Father . . ."

But I didn't know what to say next, and my eyes popped open. The back of my door still bore the scars from the morning Dad left. *Dear Father.* I'd always started prayers that way, and I used to have no problem imagining God as a loving father. At the time, I had a loving earthly father. But now, his betrayal left me feeling as though God had betrayed me too.

That's not true, Tessa, I told myself. *You can still trust God, even if you can't trust your dad.*

But instead of trying to pray again, I lay on my bed and sobbed until sleep rescued me from my sadness.

Chapter
13

WHEN I AWOKE THE NEXT MORNING, I smelled something weird. Pleasant, but odd. I pulled my Northside hoodie over my wild bed head and traipsed downstairs to investigate.

Mom stood in the kitchen. Not only was she not on the couch, she was also dressed in capri pants and a linen shirt. Her hair wasn't just brushed, but it was pulled back in a low, chic ponytail. The TV was off, the coffeepot gurgled to a finish, and that odd smell? Blueberry muffins.

How long had I been asleep?

She caught sight of me and smiled before saying, "Hey, pretty girl."

I stood in the doorway and watched in shock for a few moments. "Hey . . ."

If Mom noticed my surprise, she pretended not to. "Did you know that today is National Blueberry Muffin Day?"

"Um, no." I pulled the sleeves of my hoodie over my hands. "I didn't."

"Me neither. I mean, I think *every* day should be blueberry muffin day, but I guess somebody decided that today was the official day," she said as she put two muffins on a plate for me and grinned. She even had on her eyeliner. "I thought we should celebrate properly."

Seeing her like this—so animated and herself—filled me with such relief that I had a weird desire to burst into tears. "Okay, great," I said instead.

I poured myself coffee and left the hazelnut creamer on the counter for Mom to use too. This moment felt fragile, like if I breathed too hard the illusion would shatter and she'd be back on the couch with HGTV.

But aside from some shadows under her eyes, Mom looked like her old, strong self as she settled across the table from me. "How was swimming last night?"

"Fine," I said with a shrug. "Normal."

Mom raised her eyebrows. "Because you always take pictures with cute boys?"

Huh? Several seconds later, I remembered the photo I'd snapped with Abraham. The heart emoji I'd added. *She'd seen that?* I slowly chewed my bite of blueberry muffin as I stared at my plate. I finally settled on saying. "Yep. Same ol', same ol'."

Mom's laugh rang bright. "Liar. But you know what? I'm so glad you took that picture. Do you know why?"

I shook my head.

"Because when I looked at that in the middle of the night, I realized that you're going to grow up whether I'm paying attention or not. And—" Mom's chin trembled for just a moment before adding, "sadly, I have *not* been paying attention these last few weeks."

My throat felt thick as I said, "Mom, it's fine. You've had a lot on your mind."

"Your dad choosing what he did is most definitely a setback." Mom cupped her hands around her coffee mug. "And I can barely think about the baby without bursting into tears." She paused, clenched her jaw for a minute, and then took a deep inhale. "But I finally realized in the early hours this morning that I don't have to let him take more from me than he already has. That there's a lot of life to enjoy. Like you. And my friends. And art. And blueberry muffins."

I swallowed the emotion that had risen in my throat. "That's a weird list."

"I think you know what I'm saying. No more couch-potato mom. I'm—" Mom cut herself off as her phone began its plinking ringtone. "Oh, that's the church counselor. I left her a message at 2 a.m. seeing if I could get in." She answered the call and pressed the phone to her ear. "Amy? Thanks for calling me back . . ."

As Mom chatted appointment options with the counselor, I smiled at the lilt in her voice. This was the first time she'd sounded like herself since before Mackenzie's goodbye party, and it felt like a balm to my wounded heart.

I artfully arranged my remaining muffin on the plate with my steaming mug of coffee in the background. I snapped the shot, mulling how I would talk up my mom in the caption. Wondering what my dad would feel as I posted more and more evidence that we were doing not just *fine* but *great* without him.

—⌇⌇—

I hadn't yet read *Snowfall in October*, but Amelia was happy to inform us all that it was about four sisters in Nazi-occupied Poland and that she'd already started to work on blocking. I didn't really know what that meant, but her copy of the script was covered in highlights and pencil notes in the margins.

The longer Amelia talked, the smaller Shay became. She'd kicked off her cowboy boots and pulled her knees tighter and tighter against her chest.

Izzy, meanwhile, was practically vibrating beside me. "Stars, this is going to be exciting!"

"When did you have time for all this?" I asked as Amelia turned to yet another page of notes she'd taken.

"My parents had a church meeting last night. They always want me to babysit the littles." Amelia stuck out her tongue and blew a raspberry as she made a thumbs-down motion. "But fortunately, it was boys, and all they ever want to do is play video games, so I had lots of time." Amelia motioned toward her script. "And we needed it. Not only am I the TA, but I'm the only one in the group with show experience."

If she would stop lording that over us all, she'd be much easier for me to like.

Izzy rocked back and forth like a kindergartner who has too much energy to sit still for story time. "Can I be Zuzanna?"

Amelia pursed her lips as if she was actually in charge of deciding. "I couldn't decide if that should be you or Tessa. Zuzanna does have a lot more lines than Maja, but—"

"Izzy can be Zuzanna, then," I said. "What are the smallest parts?"

"There are no *small* parts, Tessa." Amelia's voice slipped into a teachery pitch. "Even actors with no lines contribute to the whole."

Izzy laughed as she pulled a pink highlighter from her backpack that matched her leggings. "I don't think Tessa is looking for show philosophy. I think she just wants to be on the stage for the least amount of time."

I glanced at Shay. "And I don't think I'm the only one."

Shay cleared her throat. "Yeah, I would also like a small part."

Amelia's mouth pursed. "Can we please agree to refer to them as 'parts with less stage time'?"

I had the sudden memory of last year's spring musical. Amelia said something I couldn't remember. Whatever it was made me wonder if she'd tried out and not gotten a part. For a girl who wanted as much stage time as she could get, it was probably very important not to think of those lesser parts as unimportant or small.

"Sure." I opened my own copy of the script to the cast list. "Please give Shay and me the parts with the least amount of stage time. And great work on the blocking."

That was the correct term, right?

"Thank you." Amelia beamed. "Then how about this? Shay, you can be Lena. She has the fewest lines."

"Sounds great."

Amelia made the note in her script. "It's less stage time, but a super-fun part. Lena is bitter over the death of their brother and desires revenge. You're the only one in the script who gets to throw a punch!"

Izzy giggled and exclaimed, "Fun!" but Shay actually looked like she was the one who'd been punched.

"I don't think . . . I can do that," Shay said.

"Of course you can," Amelia dismissed her before adding, "We'll practice of course, and you'll be great."

Shay visibly swallowed and glanced at me with a pleading look, but Amelia didn't notice and had already moved on.

"Tessa, you can be Maja."

I skimmed the short list of characters with their description. Maja: The bright, optimistic one who tries to help her sisters see everything through her own rose-colored glasses.

I groaned. "Can't I throw a punch too?"

Amelia carried on as if I hadn't spoken. "Izzy will be Zuzanna, the eldest sister. Zuzanna hasn't been the same since her fiancé was taken away by the Nazis. He's presumably at a concentration camp and Zuzanna is nearly sick with worry over her beloved Patreek."

"Oh, my stars, that'll be so fun. I'm going to picture him as this supercute boy on my sister's robotics team." Izzy pressed a hand to her forehead, closed her eyes, and gusted a dramatic "Oh, my long-lost Patreek!"

I couldn't help giggling at her theatrics, and even Shay chuckled. Amelia, however, frowned as she considered Izzy, as though she doubted this casting choice.

"It's not a soap opera, Izzy." Amelia cleared her throat. "And I'm the main character, of course. Aleksandra, who works tirelessly and thanklessly to care for her sisters. Now that we have casting out of the way, let's talk sets."

Amelia turned her MacBook toward us and scrolled through so many set variations that my attention waned. She'd created a Pinterest board for *Snowfall in October*, as if this was actually something more than a class assignment.

While we waited for the eighth option to load, I asked, "Exactly how long was that church meeting?"

Amelia's laugh had a bite of resentment. "I've learned to never underestimate how long these things will last. I'm kinda used to it by now. Our house is a revolving door of families from church. They come for counseling, or meetings, or Bible study, or whatever. Why's the Wi-Fi being so slow?"

"What church do you go to?" Izzy asked as she braided a small strand of her hair.

"River of Life." Amelia clicked refresh a couple of times on the page. "I've gone there my whole life. Here we go, it's *finally* loading."

"Honestly, Amelia, whatever you think is best for the set is probably fine with all of us." I flipped the page of my script and highlighted another Maja line. There weren't a ton of them, for which I was grateful, but each one was so stupidly optimistic, I thought about asking Shay if she'd trade parts with me. Probably not, since Maja appeared to have twice as many lines as Lena. "According to the grading rubric, Ms. Larkin doesn't expect lavish sets."

"Maybe not, but sets are so fun. Why would we settle for something mediocre?"

"Uh, because we have lives?"

"I'm the TA—"

"You are?" I made a small gasp of feigned shock. "I had no idea."

Izzy's giggle sounded nervous, and Shay looked away.

Amelia laughed, though it sounded a bit staged. "Ha ha, Tessa. All I was going to say is that because of my unique role, my group needs to really shine."

I rolled my eyes at my script. I didn't even care if she saw and her feelings were hurt. I was so sick of her bragging, and I resented having to play some dumb part in a play when I should be going to Iceland with Dad. Who should still be married to Mom.

"Amelia, how about you show us your top three and then we vote?" Shay suggested. "You obviously know way more than any of us about this kind of stuff."

Amelia frowned at the screen and prattled on about the merits of options two and eight. Izzy was the only one who engaged with her, and pretty soon it was just the two of them talking.

"I don't know about you," I murmured to Shay as I highlighted another inanely optimistic line of Maja's, "but this whole One Act thing looks like the worst."

Shay nodded with more enthusiasm than I'd seen yet from her. "I don't think I can do this," she admitted. "How did I even wind up in this class?"

"I've been asking myself this every single day."

"Really?" Shay's shoulders relaxed. "I thought I might be the only one who wants to vomit at the thought of getting up onstage."

"We'll bring a trash can up there for both of us."

Shay's laugh was husky and low as she flipped the page of her script.

"So where do you live?" I asked conversationally as the bell rang.

Amelia closed her computer. "Good thing we have lunch next and can keep talking about this!"

I refrained from making another sarcastic comment. Shay glanced at me and smiled, like she'd heard it anyway.

As we went through the lunch line, Izzy murmured to me, "So that seems to be an everyday thing now."

I thought she meant the salad I was assembling, but when I looked at her, she bobbed her head toward the tables. Toward Alex's table. Lauren was there, of course, and today they were actually sitting by each other.

"Yeah." I pushed down the spike of jealousy that rose up. "They're going to homecoming together. Alex told me last night."

Izzy growled, and I shrugged.

"How did he act when he told you?"

I reached for a bottle of lemonade. "I don't even know what that means."

"Like, was he excited? Nervous? Hesitant?"

"He was . . . Alex. Levelheaded. Just passing information along, one friend to another."

Izzy growled again. "I really don't think he likes her. He treats her the same way he treats me."

I frowned. "What does that mean? Alex likes you."

"He's always very nice, but he's different with you. More . . . I don't know. Warmer. More tender."

I wanted to wrap her observation around me like a fuzzy blanket. Instead, I shrugged the words away. "It's just because we've known each other forever."

"Maybe. But I think Lauren's asking for heartbreak."

"I know Alex. If he didn't want to go with her, he would've said no."

"Well . . ." Izzy sounded hesitant. "You know him better than I do."

The conversation dropped while we scanned our lunch cards,

but I couldn't ignore the way she kept looking at me like I might fall apart at any moment.

"I'm not upset about it," I said as we walked to what had become our usual lunch table. Shay sat alone there, but Amelia's lunch tray occupied another space. "You don't have to keep looking at me like I'm about to shatter."

"But you know it would be okay to be upset, right?" Izzy's words were gentle. "You don't have to be fine with it, Tessa."

Her kindness lured a piece of truth out of me. "I'm not exactly fine with it, but I have bigger things going on right now. My parents, I mean."

"Oh. Yeah, that makes sense."

Izzy cast me one last sympathetic look, and then we joined Shay at the table.

"Where's Amelia?" I asked.

Shay crunched into her apple. "She picked up the wrong phone in Drama. Here she comes."

I looked behind me as Amelia came rushing back, hair bouncing behind her, iPhone clutched in her hand. "Okay," she said breathlessly as she collapsed in her seat. "Back to talking about sets. Wait, where's my laptop?"

Usually I found it annoying when Amelia couldn't find something, but this time it made me laugh.

"Under your lunch tray," I said.

"Well, who put it there?" she joked as she moved her tray.

I felt a warmth in my chest as I realized despite Amelia's annoying traits—her forgetfulness, her boasting—I genuinely liked her. I genuinely liked all three of these girls, actually. And I felt glad—just a little bit—that I was accidentally put in Intro to Drama.

Chapter
14

MACKENZIE GAZED INTO THE SCREEN, looking tired. "It's not *bad*, exactly. It's just different."

The wall behind her was coral, with a honey-oak shelving unit only halfway in the shot. Not recognizing the scene behind her felt strange. *And was I imagining that she looked thinner?*

"The pictures look nice."

"Yeah." Mackenzie fussed with a strand of hair. "Great 'gram content. That's what Florida has going for it."

I frowned at the screen. "That can't be all. Surely there are some nice people at school."

"If there are, I haven't found them yet."

"Are they mean?"

"Not *mean*. Just . . ." Mackenzie shrugged and continued, "Indifferent, I guess. I walk the halls, I go to class, I eat lunch, and I swear nobody even looks at me. It's like I don't exist."

"You exist, I promise," I said with a smile, hoping she'd return it. But she didn't.

"They just ignore me. There's no Tessa Hart in Palm Beach making sure I have someone to sit with at lunch. I miss Riverbend so much."

"What about your cousins?"

"Different friends, different school, different life. I really don't see much of them now that school has started."

I should've been calling and texting her more these last few weeks. I'd just been so caught up in my own drama. That was why I'd called her tonight, even—to tell her about the stuff going on with Dad and Rebecca, not to find out how she was doing. *What kind of friend was I?*

"Maybe you could come visit." I pulled my swim bag onto my lap. "Tell your mom it's what you want for Christmas."

"She's so distracted taking care of my grandparents. She probably wouldn't even notice if I was gone."

"You know that's not true." I riffled through the contents of my bag, reassuring myself that all my necessities for practice were in there.

"Though if I move back, I'll have to watch Noah and Leilani together." Mackenzie wrinkled her nose. "It's bad enough seeing their relationship unfold on Snap."

I'd barely been on Snapchat recently, except to respond to whatever Amelia had sent to our drama group. "Are they together?"

"Basically." Mackenzie wagged her head, the way she always did when fighting off tears. "I don't know how you stomached Leilani and Alex last year. I really don't."

I stopped multitasking and set my bag aside. I wanted to tell her that losing Noah didn't merit tears, but I doubted that would be helpful. "It's not a good feeling, is it?"

"The worst," Mackenzie moaned. She wiped her cheeks with the sleeve of her hoodie. "And even when Noah and I were dating, I thought he maybe liked her, but I didn't think she would betray me and date him. Especially after how he dumped me."

I didn't know what to say to that, so I just nodded and said, "I know."

Mackenzie sniffled. "I'm glad you're moving on, though. Who's that hot, shirtless guy in the swim cap I saw on your Insta? You've never mentioned him before."

"Oh, Abraham. He's no one." I hoped my blush didn't betray me. "I mean, he's someone. Obviously. He's on my swim team. We were just being goofy."

"Sure you were." Mackenzie smirked. "Like it didn't cross your mind that Alex might be writhing in jealousy when he saw that."

I'd actually been thinking more about my dad and hoping he'd hate it. Before I could respond, Mackenzie squealed, "Tessa! I didn't even see this comment Abraham left. 'You're the cutest.' Somebody's flirting with you."

I rolled my eyes. "Abraham is a chronic flirter. I don't think he even knows when he's doing it. I mean nothing to him, I promise."

"I dunno." Mackenzie held her phone to the screen on her laptop, showing me the picture of Abraham and me. "I'm sensing some chemistry."

"If there is, it's one-sided." The doorbell rang and I glanced at the clock. "I gotta go. Youth group and then swim team tonight. I'll call you tomorrow, Mackenzie?"

"Sure." Mackenzie shrugged and said, "Not like I have anything on my schedule."

I hesitated a moment, watching my friend as she picked at her cuticles. I was used to Mackenzie's mood swings. I'd just caught her in a moment when the pendulum was down, that was all. She'd be back up within the hour, I was sure of it.

"I'll call you," I promised once more. "Bye."

The doorbell rang again as I thundered down the stairs. Duke Ellington music vibrated from Mom's basement studio, so I was positive she hadn't heard Izzy ring.

I whipped open the door. "Sorry, I was on the phone." I noted the plate of blue cupcakes in her hand and laughed. "Do you even need an occasion, or do you just bake constantly?"

Izzy frowned. "They're to cheer you up, of course. That's why I picked waves."

Upon closer examination, I saw the white wave pattern on each cupcake. "Do I need cheering?"

Izzy's frown deepened. "Didn't you see Lauren's video on Instagram this afternoon?"

My stomach reacted with that whoosh feeling, like when you start down a massive drop on a roller coaster. "No . . ."

"It's a homecoming makeup tutorial. She tagged Alex as her date. I thought you might be upset."

At least it wasn't an Alex-is-my-boyfriend-now kind of post. Not that I was still naïve enough to think that wasn't coming. Not like last year when I'd thought Leilani was just his homecoming date.

I opened the door wider for Izzy to come inside. "A homecoming makeup tutorial? She's really into Instagram."

"Yeah. She told me she gets most of her makeup for free because of the tutorials she does. I'm thinking about posting more tutorials on my IGTV and seeing if I can get some baking stuff for free." Izzy glanced around the entryway of my house. "This looks like a place where I should take my shoes off."

"If my dad still lived here, absolutely. I don't think Mom cares as much."

Izzy tugged off her canvas slip-ons anyway. "Your house is really nice."

"Thanks." My stomach squirmed as I attempted to look at it through Izzy's eyes. Our house had been a little ridiculous for three people, but for two? Now it just seemed stupid. We had almost three times as many bathrooms as people who lived here.

I led Izzy to the kitchen, and then called down the basement stairs. "Mom? We need to go soon!"

I wasn't sure she could hear me over the music, but after a moment I heard a muffled, "'Kay, be right up."

I rolled my eyes at Izzy. "Five bucks says I'll have to call for her again."

Izzy tweaked several cupcakes on the plate. "What's she doing?"

"She teaches art classes in our basement, so she's probably getting everything set up."

"Ooh, art classes?" Izzy's eyes sparked. "Maybe I could take a class sometime."

I laughed and lifted a cupcake off the plate. "You want to take an art class from my mom?"

"Sure. I've never talked to a real artist before. Think she'd let me join?"

"Probably." I peeled back the wrapper. "But I thought you did baking stuff."

Izzy shrugged and said, "I'm still trying to find my niche. I mean, I love baking. And I have been focusing my Instagram on food—baked goods, mostly—and it's doing pretty well. But I love art too, so maybe I could make another account for art. Or start a YouTube channel!"

"Maybe you need a plan of some kind." I nudged the plate toward her.

Izzy peered at the cupcakes. "Is it rude to eat a cupcake that you gave to somebody else?"

I shrugged and said, "If you don't, then I'm rude for eating in front of you, right? Don't make me be rude, Izzy."

"Well, okay," Izzy said with fake hesitation. "I tried a different buttercream frosting. Tell me what you think."

"I think—" I paused to lick extra icing off my finger "if there was a way for everyone who followed your Instagram to taste your cupcakes, you would get a show on Netflix."

"Stars, you're the best." Izzy clapped with delight and gave me a hug. "So I never know how to bring this up, but how are things going with your parents?"

My heart stuttered. "Um, bad."

Izzy pouted. "Are they in counseling or anything?"

"No."

I needed to just tell her. Izzy was a good-enough friend to trust with the truth.

"Maybe some space will be good for them, and they'll realize how much they miss each other . . ."

Izzy trailed off as I shook my head. I laughed, but it had a bitter edge to it. "That would be nice, but my dad is living with his girlfriend, and—"

Izzy's mouth fell open dramatically in a way that reminded me of Amelia. "*Qué*? No way."

I looked at my cupcake as tears pricked my eyes. "Yeah, and . . . the best news? She's pregnant," I said sarcastically.

Izzy gasped. Her dark-brown eyes went wide. "Oh, Tessa . . ."

I bit back the urge to say it was fine. "Labor Day weekend was kinda messed up."

"Well, yeah." Izzy seemed too stunned to move. "I wish you'd told me sooner."

"You're actually the first person I've told." I thought about saying more. Like how kind she was to me, and that I was glad we were becoming friends. Instead I shoved the remainder of my cupcake in my mouth.

"I won't tell anybody this time."

I nodded. I believed her.

"Tessa, I feel terrible that I haven't been praying about this for you." Izzy shook her head, as if scolding herself. "I can be so self-involved sometimes. But I'll start praying every day, okay?"

"Izzy, don't feel bad about that. It's not like your prayers would've changed anything."

Izzy's frown deepened. "What do you mean? I know praying

about something isn't a guarantee that it'll happen, but of course it could change things. Why would God ask us to do something if it wouldn't change anything?"

Prayer had always been a bit confusing for me. It seemed like a no-lose situation for God. If we prayed for something and it happened, we were supposed to give praise to God for His blessings. If we prayed for something and it didn't happen, then we always chalked it up to not being God's will. But those didn't seem like good, Christian thoughts to voice.

Instead I said, "I just mean that some things can't be undone. This baby is coming no matter what I pray."

"Well, yeah. But the Bible says that nothing is too difficult for God." Izzy infused her voice with confidence. "That faith the size of a mustard seed is capable of moving mountains. I know this feels like an impossibly big mountain, Tessa, but I believe God could move it and help you forgive your dad. Maybe even heal your parents."

Izzy smiled at me in a kind, encouraging type of way.

I tried to smile back. Tried to hold eye contact. "Yeah, you're right. Thanks."

Izzy was so sweet and innocent. *How could I expose to her those dark thoughts in my heart? That I hated my dad. That forgiving my dad for what he'd done to us didn't even feel like a mountain I wanted God's help with moving. I liked being angry. He didn't deserve my forgiveness. He'd never even asked for it.*

And if I stopped being angry with my dad, then I would be left just feeling hurt. Being angry was so much easier.

Chapter
15

"But, Zuzanna, the sun is shining today. Let our hearts be happy."

"Cut," Amelia called, and it was all I could do *not* to throw my script at her. "Tessa, you do not sound like your heart is happy. You sound like you're reading lines."

I waved my script in the air. "Gee, I wonder why?"

Amelia fixed me with a patronizing look. "You're supposed to rehearse like you want to perform. Try to *not* read the lines."

"But I don't know my lines yet—"

"You do." Amelia put her hands on her hips. "You're using your script as a crutch."

"What? No, I'm not. If I don't say them just right, Izzy won't know her cue."

"Let's just keep going." Izzy combed through the ends of her hair. "Claire will be here in ten minutes to pick me up."

"Fine." Amelia, our self-appointed director, waved us on. "Take it from Zuzanna's line. And Izzy, it's not a soap opera. Bring it down a notch or two."

Early in rehearsal, I snapped a couple photos of us and posted them on Instagram—*would those make it look to my dad like I was thriving in my new normal?*—but smiles had quickly vanished after that as Amelia nitpicked every move we made.

Our performance was less than two weeks away, and Amelia was like one of those wind-up toys. With each passing day, it was as though her gears tightened another notch. I'd agreed to staying after school for an hour today in hopes that it would wind her motor down, but so far there'd been no noticeable difference.

Izzy seemed to have no trouble taking direction from Amelia. She nodded, took notes, and ate up every tidbit of advice Amelia threw her way like it was wrapped in bacon. Shay didn't seem bothered by Amelia's corrections either, but they weren't making an impact on her performance. Her character was full of passionate anger, and poor Shay was so quiet she just couldn't seem to channel an ounce of feeling into her words. She sounded like Alexa reading an audiobook to us. Not that I was judging.

If I hadn't already memorized most my lines, I would have suggested we switch parts because I hated my character. Stupid Maja just wanted to bury her head in the sand and pretend Nazis weren't doing terrible things all around her. My annoyance with her naïveté kept bleeding through my lines, though it probably didn't matter. Even my best wasn't good enough for Amelia, and I could understand why. Amelia was a spectacular actress. The awe I felt every time she took the stage only annoyed me further.

"Tessa, it's your line." Amelia didn't bother to restrain her irritation.

"Sorry." I skimmed my script. "I know, Zuzanna, but Patreek wouldn't want you to be sad like this. He would want you to be out running barefoot through the grass and picking wildflowers."

Amelia groaned. "Tessa, you've been happy before, right? You know what it sounds like when people are expressing happy thoughts?"

"I have the dumbest character." I planted my fists on my hips, crunching my script. "Why can't she just admit that the world is falling apart—that *her* life is falling apart—instead of trying to convince everyone around her that everything is fine?"

From below the stage, Amelia and Shay blinked up at me.

"I know you can do this, Tessa." Amelia infused her voice with confidence. "All you need—"

"Would you let up?" I snapped. "You might just have to accept that I'm terrible at this, okay?"

The multipurpose room went still. Amelia's eyes widened with shock at my sharp tone.

I swallowed. "I'm sorry. I didn't mean to lose my patience."

"No, I'm sorry," Amelia said softly. "I didn't mean to push you so hard."

My heart seemed to pound in my ears. I couldn't believe I'd snapped like that. *What was wrong with me?* "I hate being bad at things."

Amelia approached the base of the stage. "You keep saying that, but I really believe you could do a good job. I think you're so focused on doing everything perfectly that you're losing the heart of the words."

"Am I supposed to focus on doing it imperfectly?" Tears pulsed behind my eyes, and I blinked them away as I bounded down the stage stairs to my backpack. I was done for the day whether it had officially been an hour or not.

"Ideally, you focus on who this character is. How you connect with her. Your unique take on who she is."

I zipped the script into my backpack. "My unique take is that she's dumb. She should just accept that the world is falling apart around her and stop pretending otherwise."

"Tess—"

"Amelia, you're a fantastic actress. But I'm not you." I slung my backpack over my shoulders and looked into Amelia's hopeful face.

"I just want to do whatever has to be done to get an A and get off the stage as fast as I can, okay?"

Amelia looked to her shoes, sparkly floral flip-flops. "Okay."

For the first time since I'd snapped, I glanced at Izzy and Shay. Both of them were packing up their backpacks, trying to be as silent as possible. I felt a slush of guilt in my stomach for making rehearsal weird for everyone.

"Hey, Shay, maybe we should switch parts," I said with a laugh that didn't quite work. "I might be more suited for that angry sister."

Shay's smile looked wary, like she thought I might verbally assault her, too.

Izzy came up behind me and gave me a hug I didn't deserve. "We believe in you, Tessa."

"Thanks." I glanced at Amelia again, wishing I could take back my words. I wriggled out of Izzy's hug. "Have a good night, girls."

A chorus of "You too" rose as I left the multipurpose room.

Only a handful of students moved around Northside at this time in the afternoon. Some were athletes, but others might have been there for after-school clubs or activities. Two cars sat in the circle drive out front and neither were Mom's, so I grabbed a seat on the bench and pulled out my phone.

I swiped away a text from my dad—Missing you, honey. Could we talk SOON?—and opened up Instagram. My post of the four of us hadn't been up long, but my dad, Mackenzie, and Alex had already liked it. Alex had even left a comment asking when the show was. Seeing likes and comments should make me feel some sense of satisfaction, but oddly it just left me feeling even more lonely.

As Mom's SUV pulled into the circle, I mentally wriggled into my turtle shell. *I'm fine. I'm totally fine.*

I put on a smile.

——∽∿∿∽——

Leilani texted me as I loaded up my backpack.

> You bringing your bf to homecoming? We have a spot for one more couple in the limo!

This was followed by a series of emojis I couldn't quite decipher.

> What boyfriend?

As I closed my locker, she responded: Hot Indian swimming guy on your Insta! Isn't he your bf?

I laughed, earning me a side-eye from the guy a few lockers down from me.

> No! Not even a little bit. And I'm not going to homecoming.

I tucked my phone in my back pocket and navigated the halls to Honors English. Lauren and Alex were already in their usual seats. I took mine as well, and Alex smiled at me. "Hey," he said, even though Lauren was talking.

I smiled at him, and Lauren carried on as though nothing had happened. "So I think we have three votes for Olive Garden. And then three for that place I can never remember the name for. That boutiquey Mexican place? La Casa or whatever."

"La Casita."

"Yes, that's it! So, what's your preference?"

"I'm really not picky," Alex said to the cadence of his thumb tapping on his desk.

"I told the girls that's what you would say," Lauren said with a warm laugh. "I just *knew* that was going to be your answer."

Weird, because Alex wasn't the type to shy away from giving his opinion. Some disliked it about him—usually others who also had strong personalities.

"Well, it's true. I really don't care."

My phone vibrated with Leilani's response.

You should make swim cap boy your BF and come to homecoming with us!

Was anybody talking about anything besides homecoming? I stared at my screen. I didn't even know how to respond to that. *Make him my boyfriend? What did that even mean?*

Another text came in. This time, it was my dad.

Hope you have a great day, Sweetie. I miss you.

I flinched and shoved my phone into my backpack. *When would texts from him stop feeling like a surprise attack?*

Alex kicked my chair and grinned at me before saying, "Hey. You didn't seem very enthusiastic when you responded to my comment yesterday about your upcoming play."

"That's because I'm not." I tried to smile and maybe got 75 percent of the way there. My mind was still churning through Dad's text. "I hate that stupid class," I admitted. "If I had it to do all over again, I would just take the second study hall."

"You seem to be making good friends in there. I recognized Millie and Izzy. I don't know that fourth girl."

"Her name's Shay." I glanced at Lauren, feeling hyperaware of her watching us have our conversation. "She's new here. Just started earlier this month. I think it's possible she despises Drama even more than I do."

Alex pushed on my chair with his foot again. "So, when's the show? You conveniently forgot to reply to that on Instagram."

"Uh, that's because it's none of your business."

Alex laughed, and the sound warmed me from the inside. "A public show is none of my business?"

"That's correct."

"You know I can find out other ways than asking you, right?"

"Alex, it sounds like Tessa doesn't want you to go," Lauren said brightly, and then punctuated her statement with a small giggle.

"If Tessa doesn't want people to know," Alex said without taking his eyes off mine, "then maybe Tessa shouldn't post about it on Instagram."

"Posting a picture of me with my friends who happen to be in Drama with me is not the same thing as inviting everyone to my show."

Lauren pulled her sunshine-colored hair over one shoulder. With a laugh, she said, "Alex, you *have* to see this," and held out her phone to him.

He took her phone, and I turned away. This time last year, I perceived an exchange like that as Alex flirting with me. Thankfully, I was too smart for that now and knew that it was just Alex being himself, not marking me as special.

If only I could outsmart the bite of pain that came from knowing this.

—⁂—

I was the only one at the lunch table Tuesday when Amelia zipped by, clutching her tray and moving like a flower-patterned bullet train.

"Amelia!" I called out when I realized she was headed the wrong way.

Amelia startled and beamed a smile at me. "Tessa! Hi! Have you seen my phone?"

"Uh, no. Maybe—"

"Doesn't matter. I have the best news ever! Presley and Brie just invited me to go help Jenna with this play they're rehearsing for Drama II! I'm so excited, you don't even know. See ya!"

Amelia zoomed away, mustard-colored cardigan flowing

behind her, before I could even process what she'd said. I took a bite of my turkey wrap—home lunch options were much better now that Mom was back to grocery shopping—and chewed slowly. I had no idea who any of those people were or why Amelia would be so excited about skipping lunch to help them.

Izzy drew close to the table, frowning. "I thought Amelia was ahead of me in the lunch line. Did she forget her phone or something?"

"I guess she's working on a Drama II project," I said with a shrug. "She seemed really excited."

The way she'd announced Presley and Brie's invite—as if she'd been asked to homecoming by her secret crush—stirred up sadness and concern. *Should she be* that *excited?*

But Amelia was a loud and excited person. That might be all this was. How weird that I would feel so protective of her.

Izzy frowned at her phone, and then set it aside. "Still no response from Shay. I hope she's all right."

"She probably just has a cold or something. She sounded a bit hoarse yesterday, didn't you think?"

"I don't know, maybe." Izzy blew on her pizza. "Do you think she likes us? I can't tell sometimes."

I chuckled. "I don't know. I think she's just shy."

"Tessa, hey!" April waved at me as she approached our table with a lunch tray. "I didn't know you were in this lunch period. I'm supposed to have third lunch, but we have a guest presenter coming in, so they said we should eat now. Can I sit with you?"

"Sure." I gestured to Izzy. "This is my friend Izzy. Izzy, this is April."

"Hi," Izzy said brightly.

April smiled and flicked her gaze up and down Izzy as she took a seat beside me. I glanced at Izzy, trying to see her as April would. April was obsessed with her own hair—which I would admit did look like it could be featured on a shampoo commercial—and would turn up her nose at the wild quality of Izzy's thick curls. She probably didn't understand Izzy's TARDIS sweatshirt. She couldn't see the panda bear leggings under the table, but those wouldn't win her over either.

Not that April's opinion of Izzy mattered to me.

"Izzy is in drama class with me, and we go to church together." I gestured to April. "And April and I have been friends since Field Day in sixth grade. We dominated the Hula-Hoop championships."

Izzy smiled in an open, let's-all-be-friends kind of way and said, "Oh, that's so fun. Stars, I'm terrible at the Hula-Hoop."

I winced at the "stars" expression.

April smiled in a dismissive way and turned to me. "Hey, you didn't tell me Alex is taking Lauren to homecoming. Why didn't you ask him?"

Izzy's smile went tight, and she turned her focus to her French fries. She'd noticed April's indifference. I felt a familiar churn in my stomach.

I shrugged, not wanting to get into it. What conversation could I start that would include Izzy too?

"You know it would be totally fine with Leilani." April popped the lid off her fruit salad. "If you asked Alex, I mean. She's totally over him. She only has eyes for Noah these days."

"Yeah, I've noticed. So has Mackenzie. When I talked to her last, she sounded pretty upset by it."

"Why should she be? She's in Florida, and they've been broken up since spring break." April pushed a grape out of the way, heading for a chunk of cantaloupe. "Do you want us to find a guy for you, Tessa?"

I glanced at Izzy, who seemed to be making herself smaller. I should really try to include her in the conversation. "Izzy, did you and Amelia decide to go together?"

Izzy had a huge bite in her mouth, so she just nodded.

"Who's Amelia?" April asked with a smile I couldn't quite read.

"Millie Bryan," I said. "Her real name is Amelia."

"Oh." April glanced at Izzy and then back at me. "I didn't realize Millie was . . ."

Was she waiting for me to fill in that statement? "Actually named
Amelia?"

April laughed. "No! I didn't know Millie was your friend." She
looked to Izzy, including her in the conversation. "I mean, good
for you."

"What's that supposed to mean?" I asked, feeling prickly.

"Well, you have to admit. Millie's not really the kind of girl
you tend to hang out with. Not that there's anything wrong with
her. She's just a bit . . ."

My face went hot, but my words emerged icy. "Just a bit what?"

"Well, um . . ." April waved her hand around in the air. "You
know." She started to mime being fat and gestured around her
head—probably alluding to Amelia's wild hair—and contorted her
mouth in a weird way, causing her to look ridiculous. "She's . . .
different."

Izzy snorted, then started laughing hysterically. Izzy's unexpected laughter clearly flustered April. She looked at me, her
face flushing. "Sorry about that. I just assumed . . ."

Before I could respond, a male voice from several tables over
called, "April!"

I turned, and some guy I didn't know waved enthusiastically.
I expected April to just wave back, but instead she called back.
"Paul! I didn't know you were in this lunch period." She stood,
scooped up her tray, and said to me, "It's Paul," and then walked
away, as if that was all that needed to be said.

Izzy watched her, and then gave me a look like she was about
to burst out laughing. "It's Paul, Tessa. What other choice does she
have?" She rolled her eyes.

I laughed. "Yeah, I guess she thought that was a sufficient
explanation."

That knot in my gut eased as I turned back to my barely touched lunch. I guess this was why I didn't hang out with April and Leilani much anymore. April's intrusion made me realize how much fun I usually had at lunch with Izzy, Shay, and even Amelia.

"Sorry she was rude to you."

Izzy shrugged, though I could tell it still stung. "You get used to it when you're a minority," she said.

I frowned. I never really thought about Izzy being a minority, but I supposed that was true. "Well, I'm sorry all the same. In middle school she was nicer, but all of last year we were drifting apart. Only I had nobody else to hang out with. I'm glad you moved here."

She looked up from the smiley face she'd drawn in her ketchup with a French fry and grinned at me before saying, "Me too."

Chapter
16

THE NEXT DAY, I sat on the love seat with my script when Izzy walked into Drama alone, her brown curls somewhat tamed in a ponytail and her legs clad in llama-print leggings.

"Hey, nice pants."

"I adore llamas." She collapsed onto the cushion beside me. "Do you think my parents will get me one this year for my birthday?"

"I don't know. What are llamas like as pets?"

Izzy shrugged and said, "Cuddly? Dunno. I have until February 2 to do some research and convince them."

"Would you pick a llama over a car?"

Izzy snorted. "If only those were my options. When's your birthday?"

I had been doing my best to forget about my birthday. "October 1."

Izzy stopped her rummaging and stared at me. "Tessa, that's next Tuesday!"

"Yep."

"That's, like, six days away."

"I'm aware, thanks."

"Why do you seem grumpy about your birthday?"

I sighed and closed my script. "Because a couple of years ago, when I was obsessed with the aurora borealis, my dad started talking about how he wanted to take me to Iceland. He went when he was sixteen. Trip of a lifetime, changed his perspective on life, etc." I made a rolling gesture with my hand. "So, my big sixteenth birthday present from my parents was supposed to be my own trip of a lifetime to Iceland with my dad. A Daddy-Daughter Duo Megadate. We were supposed to fly to Iceland the Saturday after my sixteenth."

"Oh."

"Yeah."

"And no chance you'll do that now?"

I felt my eyes prickle. "Nope. I can barely handle talking to him, so an international trip together doesn't sound great."

Izzy wrapped me in a side hug. "I'm so sorry. I don't even know what to say."

I shrugged and thought, *Me neither*. "Why are we still the only ones here?" I said. "Where's Amelia?"

"I'm guessing she's trying to figure out where she left her phone." Izzy shook her head, sending her bushy ponytail swinging. "I swear this happens every single day. Usually it's just in the bottom of her backpack. I don't know where she left it today."

"And Shay must still be sick. Did she ever respond to your text?"

"No. She didn't respond to Amelia's Snaps last night either."

"Well, neither did I, and I'm not sick."

Amelia came into the room, hair flying and expression sour. She greeted us with, "Apparently I left my phone in second period, but some idiot turned it in to the lost and found, so I had to go all the way up to the office." Amelia flopped onto the bright-pink beanbag chair. "What'd I miss? Where's Shay?"

"We don't know." Izzy rummaged in the bottom of her backpack for something. "I'm going to text her at lunch, because—"

"She didn't respond to those Snaps last night." Amelia flipped violently through her own backpack but paused to glower at me. "Though you didn't either."

"They weren't time critical, were they? I was at swim—"

"Of course you were at swimming." She dropped her glower and returned to whatever it was she was doing in her backpack. "That's all you ever do."

Izzy's dark eyes went wide, but I felt my own narrow.

"Should I not go to swimming in case you decide to send me Snapchats about traditional Polish dresses?"

"And you're making a joke out of it." Amelia pulled a plastic grocery sack from her backpack. "Why am I not surprised? Would it kill you, Tessa, to take this class even the slightest bit seriously?"

A surly response crouched on my tongue, ready to pounce, but I caged it in with my clenched jaw.

"Is something wrong, Amelia?" Izzy asked. "You seem stressed."

"Okay, kiddos," Ms. Larkin addressed us as she strode across the rug, her black, bohemian skirt swishing. "I want everyone to spread out. Get into a comfortable spot either on the furniture or the floor where you can do some thinking."

This sounded potentially painful.

"Boys," Ms. Larkin called as students shuffled around the room. "We can't have two in the stiletto chair. One of you will need to relocate, thank you."

With a huff Amelia rearranged her pink beanbag chair. "Yeah, I'm stressed. Our One Act is in ten days. Ten! The only ones who care are you and me."

"Oh, I don't think that's true," Izzy said gently as I snapped, "What? Just because my way of caring looks different than *your* way of caring—"

"Tessa, voice off, please."

My face flamed at Ms. Larkin's reprimand, and I looked into my lap with tears spiking. I couldn't remember the last time a teacher got onto me for talking when I shouldn't be.

"I know you're all eager to rehearse your plays, but we're going to spend these first ten minutes practicing feeling emotions. Some of these will be uncomfortable for us. That's okay." Ms. Larkin smiled at all of us before continuing, "That just means you're doing it right. I want you to all close your eyes."

Ms. Larkin took a seat in one of the soft armchairs and closed her eyes too. "Let's start with a comfortable one. Think of a time when you felt very happy."

I squirmed on the love seat and tried to nudge away the shame of being called out in front of everybody for doing the wrong thing.

Happy. When had I last felt really happy? Definitely not in the last six weeks. I guess that time I convinced Kayleigh to get in the water at the preseason meet was the last time I remembered feeling pure happiness.

"Let your mind soak in the memory." Ms. Larkin's voice had the soothing quality of the meditation app my mom used sometimes. "Use your senses to recall the scene. Who was there with you? What could you smell?"

A stifled chortle of laughter came from a section of boys. Probably the same boys Ms. Larkin had to tell not to share the stiletto chair. Though practically in the next breath, Ms. Larkin had to correct me, too. Shame pushed its way back into my thoughts.

Ms. Larkin pressed on. "Could you taste anything? What did it sound like in that place? What time of day was it?"

One part of my brain ticked off the right answers—chlorine, loud, early evening—while the other wandered to the party I'd thrown that night. *How stiff and weird my mom had been. How my dad had acted like nothing was wrong. Right now, I should be packing for Iceland. Had Dad been able to get a refund on the tickets? Was he holding out hope that I'd change my mind?*

"Now, think about how your body responded to feeling happy." *Oh, that's right. Happy. I was supposed to be thinking happy thoughts.*

"Was your heart pounding, or was it at rest? Was your body in motion somehow?"

For about two seconds I recalled Kayleigh's arms looping around my neck, and then the thoughts were crowded out by how much money those tickets had been. *Maybe Mom and I could go instead? Surely after what he'd put us through, Dad wouldn't bat an eye at the fee to change the plane ticket to Mom's name. She hated flying but maybe—*

"Okay, everyone." Ms. Larkin's voice had a chipper, singsong quality. "Open your eyes. In the One Acts, who of you are playing characters who are predominately happy or optimistic?"

A few hands went up. Not until Amelia shot me a look did I realize mine should be one of them.

"Did you all learn something that you could bring to your character?" Ms. Larkin smiled at us all expectantly, so I just nodded. "Wonderful!" she exclaimed. "Now let's try something a bit more complex. Everyone close your eyes again."

I supposed it wasn't a total lie. I had learned that we shouldn't have cast me as Maja.

—m—

When we'd finished "accessing our emotions" for the day and were released to rehearse our plays, Izzy and Amelia both shifted on their beanbag chairs to face me on the love seat.

Amelia kept her gaze cast onto her lap. "Sorry I was grouchy with you earlier."

"Happens to all of us," I said. "It's fine. Sorry I didn't respond to your Snaps last night. I meant to, but—"

Amelia waved away the rest of my apology. "Swimming is a bigger deal to you than theater. I get it."

"It is," I said slowly, "but that doesn't mean that I don't care about the show. That's why I'm working on memorizing my lines in every spare moment."

"You are?" Amelia brightened and her shoulders straightened. "Okay, good. Because it seemed like you weren't making any progress on that and you should really be off-script by now."

"I'm basically off-script." But I definitely preferred to read from it. Looking other people in the eyes when I said my lines felt far too vulnerable. If I said that, though, I'd be admitting Amelia was right. The script was my crutch. "Those few lines that are in Polish trip me up."

"Same here." Izzy pulled a Starburst package from her backpack and offered them around. "My mouth just can't make those sounds."

"Just get close, I say." Amelia selected a red Starburst. "No one in the audience knows Polish either."

"You can't know that for sure. Thank you, Izzy." I unwrapped a pink square. "What if we have somebody who speaks Polish in the audience, and I deeply offend them by saying the wrong words?"

"I think you're better off faking the Polish and focusing on sounding like you're not reciting lines. Was the exercise Ms. Larkin led helpful?"

"Oh, yeah." I gave her a flat smile to match my dry voice. "I'm ready to be a ray of sunshine on the stage."

Amelia frowned. "I can't tell if you're being funny or not."

"Happy is a tough emotion for me these days."

I instantly regretted my words. Now Amelia would ask why happiness was tough for me, and then I would have to go into the gory details of my parents and the pregnancy. Especially now that we were good enough friends, I would feel bad about lying. I really, really didn't want to cry in drama class. I braced myself to ease out of my turtle shell.

"Oh, I so get that," Amelia said on a sigh. "Ever since my brother got married, I've felt mildly depressed."

Oh, okay. She was going to make my admission about her. That was good. I hadn't wanted to talk about my parents' divorce anyway. I slid back into my turtle shell. I should feel grateful, but instead I felt oddly annoyed. As if some secret part of me had actually *wanted* to open up about my dad and Rebecca and the baby.

"Do you not like his wife?" Izzy asked Amelia as she unwrapped another Starburst.

"No, she's nice. I just miss having him at home. When Josh lived there, I had somebody to hang out with. My parents are always hosting people, or planning to host people, or cleaning up from hosting people. They don't have room for me. Not that I would hang out with them anyway, I guess."

"Don't you have a sister?" Izzy asked.

"Maggie. She's in the first year of approximately one million for med school."

"Well, you can hang out with us." Izzy offered the package of Starbursts again. "And you have your friends in Drama II, right?"

At the mention of the Drama II friends, Amelia's face took on the expression she'd worn that day when she came into Drama I. The I-just-smelled-something-terrible expression. "Yeah, we're kinda friends, I guess. They're older. You know how it is."

I frowned. "How old are they?"

"Well, Presley and Brie are sophomores, I guess. But Jenna's a junior."

"Did the project you guys were doing yesterday not go well?"

"Whatever, it's fine," Amelia said in a way that made me think it was absolutely not fine. "Ooh, Shay just sent a Snap!"

"Amelia," I groaned as she hid her phone beneath her script. Ms. Larkin had her back to us, thankfully.

"Says she'll be at school tomorrow. She's been sick. Bummer."

"That's sad." Izzy tucked her package of candy back into her backpack. "I wish she'd said so sooner. I would've taken her chicken noodle soup or something. Not that I know where she lives. Or that I would have a way to get it to her."

"You know Booked Up?" Amelia said as she typed. "That's where she lives."

That didn't sound right. "She lives at the bookstore?"

"Her aunt is the owner, and Shay lives in the upstairs apartment with her."

"Oh, my stars, that sounds amazing." Izzy kicked off her shoes and propped up her feet on the love seat. "But why doesn't she live with her parents? Did something happen to them?"

Amelia put her phone away, much to my relief, and said with a shrug, "She didn't share, and I didn't ask. That's all I know." She reached for her backpack with an exaggerated groan that drew the attention of several nearby groups. "Should we work on the play? I brought costume ideas."

She said "costume ideas" like it was a line from a show tune and made jazz hands.

Izzy clapped with delight, and I forced a "Yay," hoping to stay on Amelia's good side.

Just ten more days, I told myself. Only it made me even sadder to think that had my dad made different choices, I would be saying the same thing but with a vastly different tone.

Chapter
17

Instead of the Hastings family's van pulling into my driveway at 5:45, it was Alex's Civic. With a flutter in my chest, I pulled my rain jacket over my head and splashed out to the car. Alex leaned across the passenger seat to push open the door as best he could.

"Thanks." I flopped gracelessly into the seat as thunder rolled in the distance. "I can't believe how soaked I got just running to your car."

He laughed as he turned the air vents my way. "This is my first time turning on the heat this fall."

I pulled my hood down. "But of course you're still in shorts."

"Well, yeah. It's just rain."

"It's fifty degrees outside."

Alex put the car in reverse. "Do you have a point?"

I rolled my eyes. "Did you guys have cross-country today or no?"

"Yeah, we did some weights and sprints in the gym. Guess that's something nice about swimming, huh? No need to cancel for a little rain."

"They still cancel for thunderstorms, so no swimming for me tonight. You'll be giving me a ride home too, if that's okay."

"Always." He grinned at me, and a zip of happiness ran up my spine. "It'll be nice to catch up," he said. "Feels like I don't see you much at school. You always have friends around."

"What? That's not true."

"Sure it is. Only chance I have to talk to you anymore is English class."

"Which is a little weird with Lauren there." The words were out of my mouth before I thought how awkwardly they were going to land. "Which is fine. Obviously. She has every right to be there."

"I know what you mean," Alex said. "It's fine."

And he really sounded like he meant it, but I longed for him to think I was 100 percent okay with Alex and Lauren. "What restaurant did you end up picking for homecoming?"

"La Casita. I guess one of her friends' dates has a gluten thing, so Olive Garden wasn't a great choice."

"That makes sense. Are you guys going in a big group or something?"

"Just a couple of her friends. So, your first big swim meet is this weekend, yeah?"

"It is." I adjusted the air vents so they wouldn't blow right in my eyes. "I'll be in Indy most of Saturday and Sunday."

"Are you coming to the game Friday?" Alex asked as he pulled into the church parking lot.

"No. Izzy has to watch her younger brother because her parents are going out to celebrate their anniversary, Amelia has some rehearsal thing for her other drama class, and Shay . . . well, she's Shay. Homecoming football game isn't a big draw for her. So I wouldn't have any friends there."

"Ouch." Alex pressed his hand over his heart. "That was painful to hear."

"You know what I mean."

"What about April or Leilani? Are you not hanging out with them at all?"

I rolled my eyes. "We just don't have anything in common anymore. They've asked me to come to a couple of parties, but it's Noah and his friends." I made a scrunched-up face, and Alex mimicked to echo his agreement.

"Yeah, you don't want to do that." He shut off the ignition. "I can't believe I liked her last year. What was I thinking?"

"That she's gorgeous?"

The interior light came on in the car, illuminating Alex's blush. "I was being pretty stupid, I guess." He looked intently at his lap. "Can you forgive me?"

"There's nothing to forgive." I kept my voice light. Kept my turtle shell snug around me. "And you made a better choice this year. Lauren isn't like Leilani."

Alex nodded but still looked away. "You could hang out with us Friday at the game, you know. If you wanted to come."

My phone buzzed in my pocket and I reached for it. "That'd be a little weird, I think. I don't know that Lauren would want me there."

"It'd be fine. Is something wrong?"

The text that had come in was from Dad.

> Talked to your mom and she says you still think
> you don't want to go to Iceland. Is that true?

"Tessa?"

I turned the phone to Alex, and he leaned forward. His hair flopped onto his forehead with the motion.

He shifted his gaze to me. "You're not going?"

I shook my head.

Alex's face looked as though *his* trip to Iceland had been taken away from him, and his show of empathy made my heart beat double time. "I get it, but you've been planning this for so long . . ."

"I hadn't really made up my mind, but then—" a weird laugh bubbled out of me—"I found out on Instagram that his girlfriend is pregnant."

Izzy had gasped and gone big with her reaction. Alex, however, leaned back in his seat and exhaled slowly. "I don't even know what to say."

The rain pounded on the windshield. Other youth group kids were being dropped off or parking their own cars. "We should head inside."

"Are you sure? Because we can talk if you want."

"Thanks, but I'm fine," I said as I typed **Yes** and sent it to my dad.

Then I pushed open the door and let the rain in.

—⁓〰⁓—

I felt as though only half of me came to youth group. I half listened to Izzy as she talked about a fit Sebastian had thrown after school. I kept zoning out when Zoe talked about hope . . . or peace . . . or something. The moment group dismissed to rejoin the boys for snacks and games, I couldn't have even told you what our Scripture was that night.

"Thanks for helping, girls," Zoe said as Izzy and I lingered after dismissal to help straighten the lounge.

"Sure!" Izzy's bright tone matched her sunshine-colored sweatshirt. The color would've looked weird on me but worked fantastic with her complexion. "Did you figure out if you can come to the play on Saturday?"

Zoe frowned. "Not this Saturday, right?"

"No, next Saturday."

I squatted to pick up a pen that had rolled under the couch. "You invited Zoe to the One Acts?" I looked to Zoe. "You do *not* have to come."

"I know," Zoe said with a mischievous smile. "I don't *have* to do anything. I would *like* to come."

Izzy jumped in place and cried, "Yay!"

Zoe laughed, and Izzy launched into details about her role as Zuzanna. After a minute, I realized my thoughts had drifted back to a swirl of Iceland and pregnant Rebecca. I tried to rejoin the conversation without anyone noticing I'd been absent, but I could tell I'd been unsuccessful by the way Zoe looked at me.

"Izzy, can Tessa and I meet you in the game room?" Zoe asked. "I need to talk to her about something."

"Oh, sure." Izzy grabbed her bag off the beanbag chair. "See you in there."

Zoe waited until the door had closed before turning to me. "I've wanted to check in with you, and now seems like a good time if you don't need to rush off."

I felt like every muscle in my body tensed, but I tried to shrug and say a casual "I don't."

She gestured to the closest sofa, and I sat. She took the other end and pulled her knees to the side so she was facing me. "How are things?"

I nodded and said, "Things are okay."

Zoe arched her eyebrows. "Other than your parents divorcing?"

I gave a nervous laugh. "Well, yeah."

"And your mom told me they're expecting a baby?"

"Uh, yeah."

"And the boy you like is taking someone else to homecoming?" She knew about Alex and Lauren too? "Uh . . ."

"Want to try that answer again?"

"Okay-*ish*?"

"You know it's okay *not* to be okay, right?" Zoe speared me with a look. "From what I've observed, it looks like you're just trying to soldier through. Is that accurate?"

I shrugged and said, "What's the other choice? Falling apart?"

"You think there's only two choices here? Be a total mess or be Wonder Woman?"

Well, it did seem a little ridiculous when stated that way. "No?"

Zoe grinned before saying, "You sound so sure. It's fine to not be fine. My parents divorced my senior year of high school, and it was the worst season of my life."

"I didn't know that," I said. "That sounds stressful."

"It was awful. It's still awful sometimes, honestly. They're both remarried, and I like their new spouses just fine, but it's weird. My stepmom is kinda similar to my mom. Like I think they would be good friends under different circumstances. I spent a lot of time trying to figure out why my parents got divorced and then remarried such similar people. And why that seems to work better for them." Zoe shook her head, as if shaking away the thoughts. "That path of questioning leads to madness, I've learned. Anytime I've started to veer down that path, I make myself come right back."

"I can't imagine. I haven't met my dad's girlfriend yet. I stalk her on Instagram. She has a ridiculous number of followers on there, actually." An unexpected swell of emotion rose up in my throat and came out as a choked laugh. "It's awful to see pictures of him looking so happy. Does that make me a terrible person?"

Zoe's smile held tenderness. "It makes you a normal person."

"When I see those, it just looks like he's unaffected, you know?"

Zoe nodded and said, "I do. Though I'm sure he isn't."

"I don't even want to be around him. My dad . . ." I bowed my head as emotion climbed up my throat. "He was always my hero. And now I just wish he'd leave me alone. He texts me every day, even though I never answer."

"Why don't you answer? Just because you don't feel like talking yet?"

I shrugged and admitted, "That's part of it. But also, that feels like the only way to get any kind of revenge. Isn't that terrible?"

Zoe was quiet. "I think it'd be fine to tell your dad that you don't want him to text you every day."

"But what should I say?"

Zoe blinked. "Is that a trick question? You say, 'Dad, I need some space. Please don't text me every day.'"

"Oh." I leaned back against the arm of the sofa. "How do you make it sound so simple?"

"It's a little easier when you're not emotionally involved." Zoe smiled before continuing. "And you should stop stalking the girl-friend on Instagram. No good can come from it."

How well I knew that. "Yeah, you're right. I don't know why I do it, because it only ever makes me feel worse."

"You know it's not real though, right? The pictures you see of your dad on Instagram." Zoe leaned forward. "That's an incomplete look at his life through the lens of a woman who wants the world to think her life is amazing. I'm guessing, if she's Insta-famous. Of course it's going to look like your dad couldn't be happier."

I considered my own social media. A picture of me with Abraham that I'd taken hoping to make my dad angry. Fun, happy pictures from a play rehearsal that I ultimately left in a huff. Pictures of blueberry muffins on the day I learned Alex and Lauren were going to homecoming together.

Zoe could be right.

The door opened, and a forty-something man with auburn hair peeked his head in. "Oh, sorry. I'm here to meet with Amy, and—" He spotted me, and recognition dawned on his face. "Hi! Tessa, right?"

Why did he look familiar to me? "Yeah . . ."

He stepped all the way through the doorway and held out his hand for me to shake. "Sorry to interrupt. I'm Phil, Kayleigh's dad."

"Oh! Of course. I knew I recognized you."

"I can tell you're in the middle of something, and I don't want to interrupt. But, Tessa, I just can't thank you enough for what you did for Kayleigh at the preseason meet."

I waved away his words, blushing. "I was happy to do it. I'm just glad to see her doing so well."

"A big part of that is being back at swimming, and that only happened because of you. Thank you."

"I was happy to."

"Well, I'll let you get back to it. Sorry again for interrupting," Kayleigh's dad said, and he backed out of the room.

When the door had closed fully, Zoe arched her well-defined eyebrows at me. "He's a big fan of yours."

I gave her a summary of what had happened, and how I wound up getting Kayleigh in the pool and down the lane. "It was pretty cool," I finished up.

Zoe smiled and her eyes glistened. With her exhale she said, "Oh, Tessa. Don't you see?"

I shook my head, confused at what might have her so teary.

"You swam for Kayleigh when she couldn't do it for herself. Don't you know that's what Jesus wants for you in this season of your life? He doesn't want you to try to get through this on your own. He wants to swim for you."

I blinked back my own tears, unsure of what to say to that. "But what does that even mean? Like on a practical just-trying-to-get-through-my-day level?"

"It can look a million different ways. It can be a friend who prays for you, or who checks in and asks you how you're doing." Zoe sat up and beamed at me. "Tessa, Jesus invited you to be hands and feet for Kayleigh. And she said yes! Now you need to open your eyes to how He's leading others to be hands and feet for you, and you need to let them in."

Chapter
18

ABRAHAM'S NERVOUSNESS SHOWED UP in the form of constant motion. He shook out his hands, shifted his weight from foot to foot, did calf raises. If I hadn't been nervous too, it would've been funny.

"It's strange to think that I was here last year, but I was *there*." Abraham pointed to the group of swimmers wearing the bright-orange swim caps of the Indianapolis Sharks. "So much can change in a year, huh?"

I did a few calf raises too as I studied my schedule written out on my arm. "I guess I saw you at meets last year and didn't even know it."

"I think I'm offended by that."

Stray hairs tickled my forehead, and I poked them up into my cap. "That I don't remember you?"

"Yeah. I definitely remember you."

"You do not." I rolled my eyes and was happy to find his flirtation hadn't elevated my heart rate in the slightest.

When I walked in fifteen minutes ago, Abraham had been locked in a flirtatious conversation with Lexi. I wouldn't be surprised to learn he'd used the same line on her.

My lack of encouragement didn't seem to bother Abraham. He just laughed and jumped in place a couple of times.

"I'm so nervous. I'm ready to just get in the pool. Let's take a picture."

"How is that a logical next step?" I asked, but Abraham snapped on his yellow Blazers swim cap and leaned his head close to mine. He held up his phone, and I smiled because I knew the shot would probably be on social within a few minutes.

Coach Shauna began to corral us into lanes for warm-ups, and Abraham breathed a sigh of relief and put his phone away.

Once warm-ups were over, I dried off, pulled on my robe, and headed to the observation deck. Mom had been a swim mom for six years now, and it showed in her cushy stadium seat, the thermos of coffee in her hand, and the backpack full of reading material and snacks.

She closed her book as I climbed over other families to get to her. "How were warm-ups?"

"Good."

"Want a snack?"

"No, I'm too nervous to eat."

"I figured." She smiled and said, "Makes me feel better to ask, though."

I skimmed the observation deck. "Are Grandma and Grandpa coming this morning? Or in the afternoon?"

"I don't know. I sent them your schedule, but I didn't ask when they planned to be here."

Mom placed a hand on my knee, and I realized it had been bouncing up and down. Funny, Alex did that sometimes too, when he felt nervous.

"Sorry. Just jittery."

"I know."

I studied my heats, written on my arm in Sharpie. The first three were close together, but the other two were in the early afternoon. We probably wouldn't be home until dinnertime. Which was fine. Not like I had anything I needed to be back for.

My fingers itched to reach for my phone and check Instagram, even though I knew it was way too early for any homecoming pictures I actually cared about. When I checked on the drive this morning, Lauren had shots of her selected makeup, and Izzy had posted a picture of her sister testing out a hairstyle on her. But Alex wouldn't have posted anything yet. *Would he at all? The dance didn't involve running or his dog, which were his primary Instagram subjects.*

Mom drew in a sharp breath, the kind you take right before you know pain is coming. "I can't believe it."

I scanned the deck and did my own sharp intake. Dad had just come up the stairs and now searched the bleachers for a seat. He held hands with Rebecca.

Mom and I both shrunk behind the family in front of us. I even covered my eyes, like I was two and believed that if I couldn't see him, he couldn't see me. My heart pounded painfully in my chest.

"I can't believe he brought her." Mom sounded as if she'd just jogged up several flights of stairs. "I can't believe he did that."

I peeked between the gray-headed couple seated in front of me and eased upright. "They're looking for seats farther to the left."

"Good," Mom said without sitting up. "I'll be grateful for small blessings."

Dad looked like his normal, straight-arrow, boring self as he mounted the stairs to an empty space in the bleachers. After seeing the two-dimensional version of Rebecca for so many weeks, it was a bit jarring to see her out in the real world. She had on annoyingly cute boots, skinny jeans, and an oversized tunic-dress-type thing in a pumpkin spice color that concealed any kind of baby bump.

The way she glanced around, looking dazed, made me think she hadn't been to many swim meets. That and the fact that they'd brought no bag of any kind. Or maybe that meant they weren't planning to stay long.

Over the PA system, they announced that swimmers in early heats should be on the pool deck.

I reached over and squeezed my mom's hand. "I'm sorry, that's me."

"Go. I'm fine." Mom had scraped off part of her lipstick from biting her lower lip. "Good luck."

I hesitated. "You can leave if you want. You don't have to stay—"

"Are you kidding me?" Mom's eyes lit. "That man is taking nothing else from me. Certainly not the pleasure of watching you compete."

I swallowed, feeling a strange mix of pride in my mother's display of strength and startled by my dad being "that man." We once had a family dinner where Mom spent the entire meal teasing Dad by calling him ridiculously mushy names. Those days were long gone.

I picked my way down the bleachers until I reached the area of the pool deck that the Blazers had claimed. *Was Dad watching me? Pointing me out to Rebecca?* In my navy racing suit and yellow Blazers cap, I looked like every other swimmer on my team, but in my turquoise robe I was easy to spot.

"I don't care how great your memory is." Coach Shauna pushed a Sharpie into Abraham's hand. "I don't care if you have a photographic memory. We write down our heats."

Abraham rolled his eyes at me and uncapped the pen with his teeth. He drew a grid on his arm, and then glanced at the one on mine. "Butterfly first, huh?"

"Yeah." I skimmed the bleachers for Dad and Rebecca.

"You nervous or something? You seem tense."

"I always get nervous before a race." And I was going to leave it at that. No talking about my stupid dad and stupider Rebecca. I blinked away tears. "What's your first event?"

"Also butterfly. Different heat, though. Obviously."

Boys and girls didn't swim against each other. "Obviously."

I spotted Rebecca's pumpkin shirt and quickly looked away.

"Are you searching for someone?"

"Who, me? No."

Abraham smirked. "Is your boyfriend coming?"

"Alex isn't my boyfriend."

"But you knew who I meant, didn't you?" Abraham chuckled but kept his eyes on his arm as he wrote. "Is he coming?"

"No." I almost added, *He's taking somebody else to homecoming*, but there was no way for that to come out without me sounding completely bitter.

Mom sat on the other side of the observation deck, but even still had angled herself away from Dad and Rebecca. She had her book open, but her shoulders looked as though an invisible, heavy load had been draped around them.

"Something's bothering you." Abraham snapped the cap back on the Sharpie. "You marched down here like you were going to war."

"Well, it's a swim meet. How am I supposed to look?"

I scanned the bleachers again, and this time Dad saw me see them. He waved and pointed to me. I turned away, anger coursing hot through my veins. *How could he show up with her without talking to me first? If I couldn't handle texting him, what would make him think I was ready for him and Rebecca to start showing up at my stuff?* I channeled my energy into not crying on the pool deck.

"Are you still going to tell me nothing is wrong?" Abraham asked with surprising gentleness.

I closed my eyes and took several breaths. I was sure my face had a pinched I-want-to-cry expression on it. "My dad showed up with his new, pregnant girlfriend. I've never met her." My voice began to rise and tighten. "And my mom is here, and my grand-parents are supposed to be here, and . . ." I swallowed down the tears that had clogged my throat. "It's just a lot."

"It is." Abraham's voice was dark, all the charm and flirtation stripped away. "It doesn't get better."

I turned away from the observation deck and dried my eyes on my towel as nonchalantly as I could. "Yours are divorced too?"

"And remarried. Or I guess they *were*. My mom split from her second husband a couple of months ago. That's why we moved to Riverbend. But yeah. She's the only one here to watch me today because she and my dad can't be grown-up enough to share space."

I tucked my towel back in my bag. "I'm sorry. That sounds awful."

The whistle blew for the first batch of swimmers to get on the starting blocks, and Abraham and I paused our conversation until the horn sounded and the swimmers were making their way down the lane.

"I'd like to tell you it gets better, but it really doesn't," Abraham said with his eyes tracking the racers. "It's every holiday, every birthday, every school event. For every notable event in your life from now on, all the family baggage will come too."

My heart sunk to my ankles as I considered this for the first time. He was right. This situation went well beyond a swim meet or two. When I graduated high school, went off to college, got married. Rebecca and their baby—my half-sibling—would be there for all of those. And if Mom remarried, he would be too.

I groaned and bent at the waist, sickened by the thought that this was the first of many. "How do you do it?" I asked Abraham. "Do you just get used to the stress?"

Abraham shrugged and tested out his goggles over his eyes. "I guess," he said. "And you look for distractions. Instead of playing board games with the family at Christmas, you play video games by yourself. You say you don't really want a birthday party this year, that you just want to go to the movies with your friends. You find ways to cope."

The swimmers from the first heat were all back in, their faces toward the board to check their times. The second-heat swimmers had climbed up on the blocks.

"You should get lined up." Abraham elbowed me. "Stick with me today, if you'd like. I'll help you cope."

—m—

Lighthearted Abraham was an excellent distraction.

Normally at a meet like this, if I had gaps between events, I might go up to the observation deck and sit with my parents. I would have a snack, listen to music, and try to tune out the noise and chaos.

But despite several long gaps between my events, I stayed down on the pool deck. I helped the newer swimmers get to their events at the right time and played stupid games with Abraham like guessing what color of goggles the swimmer who walked by next would be wearing.

I let myself glance up to the observation deck a few times. Grandma and Grandpa had arrived, and they sat by Dad and Rebecca. Mom mostly stayed hunched over, reading, unless I was about to take the blocks. Then she stood at the edge of the observation deck half-wall, ready to cheer me on.

I hated that Dad, the one who cheated, was the one with the entourage. How was that fair?

When I swam the last of my events, I was more than ready to get out of there. I pulled my robe around me, gathered my damp towels into my swim bag, told the dwindling number of teammates that I would see them tomorrow, and took off for the locker room.

Instead of going up to the observation deck, where I would

have no choice but to acknowledge Dad and Rebecca's presence, I decided to exit into the foyer and call Mom from the parking lot.

I pushed out the locker room door to find Dad, Rebecca, Grandma, and Grandpa standing there waiting for me, as if they'd known my plan.

I had the childish instinct to turn and hide in the locker room.

Grandma opened her arms to me. "Tessa, you were amazing, as always."

As we hugged, I closed my eyes. Otherwise I would have to look at Dad and Rebecca. "Thanks, Grandma. Thanks for being here."

"Oh, we wouldn't miss it!" Grandma squeezed me hard before releasing me.

Grandpa gave me a side hug and said a quiet, "Great work, honey."

I hung on to him longer than normal because when I let go, I would have to acknowledge Dad and Rebecca.

I expected Dad to reach out for a hug or to somehow make a show of being Mr. Super Great Dad. Instead, he, too, hung back, a self-conscious smile on his face and his hands tucked in his pockets.

"Great work, Tessa," he said.

I looked away.

"This is Rebecca," Dad continued. "Rebecca, this is Tessa."

"Hello, Tessa." She had a higher voice than I expected. "So nice to meet you."

My stomach twitched, alerting me that I was not doing the right thing. That the right thing was to say that it was nice to meet her too. To look her in the eyes and shake her hand.

After an uncomfortable beat, she added, "Your dad talks about you all the time. He's so proud."

I stared at my toes, which had a few flakes of nail polish on them that I hadn't bothered to chip off. Lauren was probably getting a pedicure and having her hair done for homecoming tonight. She probably never left the house without her toenails done.

"I don't think he's very proud of you," a voice that sounded a lot like mine said. "He never mentioned *your* name until six weeks ago."

Their faces looked as if I'd splashed them all with cold water.

The words *I'm sorry* pushed to get out of my mouth, but I bit them back. They were just a habit, because I *wasn't* sorry. If anybody deserved to get an *I'm sorry*, it certainly wasn't Dad or Rebecca. They owed *me* an *I'm sorry*, and I should get to say whatever horrible thing I wanted. Guilt-free.

"Tessa," Grandma said on a shocked exhale.

I broke out of Grandpa's side hug and scurried away toward the safety of my mother. With only two events remaining in the afternoon session, most of the spectators had cleared out. Mom had been reading but looked up as I surged up the bleacher staircase. Her frown told me that my emotions were all over my face.

"What happened?"

I just shook my head. If I opened my mouth, I would bawl. *He never mentioned your name until six weeks ago.* How could those words have actually come out of my mouth?

"Is this because of your breaststroke time?"

I shook my head again. "I can't talk about it."

"Okay." Mom stood and gathered her bags. "You know, it seems kinda silly to drive all the way back to Riverbend just to be back here tomorrow at 7:30. I'm going to see if that hotel down the block has a room. How does that sound?"

The next time I stayed in a hotel, it was supposed to be in Reykjavík. Not some characterless hotel in suburban Indy. "I'm fine. We can drive home."

Mom lowered her voice, even though there weren't many people around to hear her. "Tessa, the thought of going back to our house, just the two of us." She broke off and shook her head. "I'm not sure I can do it."

Mom had been holding herself together all day; I could see the effort of it on her face now. She didn't want to drive all the way to Riverbend and *then* fall apart. And maybe she wanted to ensure that I would stay close. Maybe with how absent I'd been during the swim meet, she thought if she took me home, I would sequester myself to my room or go out with friends.

"Okay," I said. "Let's check in to the hotel."

———※———

I thought both Mom and I would explode when we got to the room. I spent the short drive to the hotel imagining my feelings swelling in my chest like a balloon, pushing up against the confines of my turtle shell. I could let them out soon. That's what I kept telling myself as the front-desk clerk went over details like Wi-Fi passwords and complimentary breakfast hours.

But when we entered the room, I instead set about hanging up my towels and suit so they'd dry by morning, while Mom brewed a cup of coffee. With the coffee brewed and the towels hung, Mom flipped on the TV and we sat on one of the beds and watched a celebrity chef make something called gâteau. I wondered if Izzy knew how to make gâteau.

At commercial, Mom asked in an empty-sounding voice, "Did you talk to them?"

I expected the question to dredge up all those heavy, weepy emotions I felt after mouthing off to Rebecca. Instead, the knot in my stomach only seemed to harden. "A little."

Mom pulled her knees to her chest, pressed her hands over her face, and began to weep. "I'm sorry. I'm so sorry, honey."

For crying in front of me? For the divorce? Did it even matter?

I leaned against her. "You don't need to apologize."

"I can't believe he brought her." Mom's words were muffled by her hands, but they did nothing to muffle her pain. "I can't believe they're having a baby."

On the TV, a teenager looked unnaturally happy about being offered a piece of gum. "Me neither," I murmured.

"And Judy and Dan sat with them." Mom's body shook with a sob, and it took me a moment to realize she meant Grandma and Grandpa. "It felt like they were giving your dad and Rebecca some kind of blessing. I was so humiliated."

I pressed closer to her. "I'm sure they just didn't know what to do. I know they disapprove."

Mom groaned. "Oh, baby girl. I'm so sorry." Strands of gray hair stuck to her wet cheeks, and she pushed them back. "I shouldn't be talking about this with you."

"It's fine, Mom. It was a hard day."

Mom gave me a watery smile as she squeezed my hand. "You've been a rock since we told you about the divorce, Tessa. I'm trying so hard, but days like today just send me into a tailspin."

I did feel very rocklike, as if my insides were carved of stone. *What would it be like to let my feelings carry me away instead of pushing them down and concealing them? What would it look like to just surrender?*

The celebrity chef whipped cream with a constant smile and muted conversation, and I watched him for a moment without really seeing. "How about if I walk to the grocery store and buy us some ice cream?"

"What would I do without you, Tessa?" Mom dug a Kleenex from her pocket and blew her nose. "At least one of us can keep it together."

—⁓—

When I awoke, I couldn't place where I was. *Why was a TV on? Why was the air conditioner so loud?*

I opened my eyes, and my location filtered back to me. The hotel by the aquatic center in Indianapolis, in a room with my mom. She breathed deeply on the other side of the bed, and I tried to roll off as gently as possible so I wouldn't disturb her.

I wanted to text Mackenzie, but the alarm clock read 2:25. Instead of the soft scenes of the seasonal, made-for-TV romantic comedy that had been on when I fell asleep, now the colors on the screen were bright and flashing as a man demonstrated how this flashlight was going to revolutionize my outdoor experience. My mouth was dry and filmy all at once, and it grossed me out that I'd fallen asleep without brushing my teeth.

I tiptoed to the bathroom, where my swimsuit was completely dry but my towels were still damp. In a few more hours, they should be dry enough to stuff into my bag.

From the front desk, I had picked up two toothbrushes and a tiny tube of toothpaste, which they kept on hand for unprepared travelers like us. I'd found myself explaining to the desk clerk that if I'd known I would be spending the night in Indianapolis, of course I would've remembered something as basic as my tooth-brush, but he seemed indifferent about the reason I needed one.

My phone was a lump in the pocket of my hoodie. I pulled it out and blinded myself with the screen by turning it on. Through bleary eyes I half looked at the Snaps that had come in from Amelia and Izzy. Their short videos and goofy pictures made it appear as though they'd found some fun at homecoming.

I saw the notification of several texts as well but didn't bother opening them and went straight to Instagram instead. The algorithm must've known what I had come here for, because Lauren's post was first in my feed.

I sank to the cold tile floor and stared.

Alex looked at me—though of course, he'd really been looking at Lauren's phone—and he was either laughing or she'd captured a really natural smile. He hadn't put extra gel or anything in his hair, like guys were prone to do for dances, and his sandy hair flopped onto his forehead. He looked like my Alex.

Or he would if I could've ignored Lauren. In another shot, she held on to one of his arms and gazed up at him, displaying her beautiful profile and elaborate updo. I couldn't tell what color their formalwear was because Lauren had put some stupid black-and-white filter on the picture, but I could tell they looked good together.

They really are a cute couple, I made myself think, because it was pointless to pretend they weren't. I was better served by dealing with this reality now, alone in a hotel bathroom in Indianapolis, than not-alone Monday morning in Honors English.

I spit toothpaste violently into the sink and scrolled through the other pictures in Lauren's series while I rinsed my mouth. One close-up of her makeup, one close-up of her hair, another group picture with Alex, and then just her and girlfriends for the remaining shots. *Huh. I expected her to post more of Alex. Maybe that was a promising sign?*

HoCo with the best people ever! 1 of 2 because I just can't help myself!

Oh . . . there were more. I clicked on her profile with a sloshy feeling in my stomach. Sure enough, the other photo series was entirely her and Alex. Alex putting on her corsage, two of Lauren putting on his boutonniere because apparently something about it was hilarious, Alex and Lauren on the front porch, Alex and Lauren in front of the fireplace, Alex holding open the car door for Lauren. And so forth.

I laid my phone down on the counter, but the images of the two of them still blazed in my mind. I stared at myself in the mirror. I still smelled of chlorine, because I'd rushed my shower, and my hair had dried in weird clumps. My eyes had the puffy not-enough-sleep look to them that they probably always did in the middle of the night.

No wonder he picked Lauren, said a nasty version of my own voice in my head. *Why would he pick you?*

My reflection blurred, and I wiped away tears with the sleeves of my Blazers swim team hoodie.

I'm fine.

This is fine.

Having a boyfriend in high school was stupid. We would just break up in a few months anyway. *Why would I want that for myself? Wasn't I smarter than that?* I definitely was, which was why I wasn't going to be jealous of Lauren or wish that Alex liked me. If I said, "I'm fine," enough, then it would become true.

"I'm fine," I whispered aloud in that bathroom. I took a deep breath and then exhaled. "I'm totally fine."

I closed out of Instagram and checked the texts. There were about seven from Izzy, giving me the blow-by-blow of homecoming. Maybe I would enjoy reading that later. One from Shay asking about my meet. That was nice. The last two were from Grandma and Dad.

Dad's was efficient. Sorry about today. I should have checked with you first about Rebecca. I won't be there tomorrow. I don't want to stress you out. Love you.

Grandma's was verbose. Tessa, I'm really sorry about how everything went today. I wish you and your father could just sit down and talk this out . . .

She rambled for several messages about how hard this all was but that we didn't gain anything by being rude to each other. I skimmed the rest and closed out of my texts.

How could I even be thinking about dating Alex as I watched my parents' marriage implode? *Even being an adult and getting married hadn't saved my mom the pain of not being picked.*

I put my phone in my hoodie pocket and crept back to bed. I turned off the glaring infomercial, sending a hush of darkness over the hotel room. Mom stirred but didn't wake.

I snuggled under the covers and lay in the blackness for a few minutes before I remembered Abraham had tagged me in something earlier, but I'd dismissed the notification without checking for details.

I could just wait until morning. Right now, I needed to go to sleep.

My willpower lasted about thirty seconds before I pulled out my phone to satisfy my curiosity.

Hanging with my fave girl in my fave city #GoBlazersINswim. Abraham had captioned a photo series that had several pictures of us together, along with a couple of just me.

I hated to think of Dad sitting in his place with Rebecca, thinking how distraught I must be over the day. *Actually, Dad, I'm doing just fine without you*, I thought as I pulled up Abraham's post. *And here's the proof.*

I reposted the goofy pool-deck pictures with cute Abraham, and then I set my alarm for a few hours later and put my phone away.

Chapter
19

AFTER WRAPPING UP MY EVENTS in the morning, Mom let me drive us home from Indy so I could log the last of the practice hours I needed to get my driver's license.

On a whim, I had packed my script for *Snowfall in October* thinking Mom might help me use car time to run lines. We made it about halfway through my first scene when Mom said, "Wait, your line reads like you're supposed to be happy."

My teeth ground together, and I gripped the steering wheel. "I know."

"Okay, so why don't you sound happy?"

"This is the best I can do."

"Oh, I don't think so. I'm sure you could infuse a little more joy into your voice. Say that last line again."

I sighed. "Zuzanna, the sun is out—"

"You're not even smiling. That's the problem. When I worked as a receptionist, that was the first thing they taught me. You should always smile when you answer the phone because the person on the other end can tell."

"I'll smile when I'm onstage, okay?"

Mom pursed her lips. "Doesn't Coach Shauna tell you guys to practice like you want to race? I think the same applies to performing onstage."

I wanted to roll my eyes at my mom, but I also didn't want to take my eyes off the road. "It's a school assignment. Ms. Larkin says we don't have to be fantastic actresses to get an A, and I'm taking her at her word. Trust me, this is good enough."

"Good enough? That doesn't even sound like you. My Tessa always wants to do her very best."

"Well, maybe my very best is that I'm a lousy actress. I can't be good at everything."

"True," Mom said, her voice mild. "Watch your speed."

Whoops. I eased my foot off the accelerator and turned on cruise control.

"Sorry," I grumbled. "I know you're just trying to help, but I promise that I'm being nitpicked adequately as it is. You know Amelia, right?"

Mom frowned. "The bigger girl who's into theater?"

"'Into theater' is an understatement. She's on my case constantly."

"Does she have a good reason to be?" Mom asked, which was completely obnoxious.

"She's a sophomore, same as me, and she critiques my performance way more than Ms. Larkin. So, no. It's just that drama is Amelia's obsession, and she can't seem to understand why I don't like it."

"You sound very worked up about this."

"Well, yeah. I have to perform this One Act thing publicly, which is horrifying. On the same day that I was supposed to be heading to Iceland. I wasn't supposed to be in Drama in the first place, and now it feels as though it's taking over my life."

"What do you mean, you weren't supposed to be in it?"

That's right. Since Mom hadn't been herself at the start of the school year, I had never shared these details with her.

I put on my left turn signal as I approached a slow-moving vehicle, checked the lane beside me, and then moved to pass.

"I signed up for Intro to Organic Farming, but something happened in the system and they stuck me in Intro to Drama instead. When I tried changing it on the first day of school, the other options were terrible. So I told myself that I needed my fine-arts credit anyway, and how bad could it be?" I laughed a sarcastic *ha ha ha*. "My stupid pride kept me from taking a second study hall. I should've taken German I or something."

Mom sat quietly in the passenger seat as I moved back over to the right lane. "What if it's not an accident that you're in the class?"

I frowned. "How do you mean?"

"I mean, I know you didn't sign up for it and want it, but what if it's where you're supposed to be nevertheless?"

"Like God wanted me in there, you mean?" Skepticism dripped from my words.

"Yeah, maybe. Or even if you can't go all the way there with me—that God orchestrated the events that put you in that class— could you at least entertain the idea that He could take something painful and uncomfortable, and make it all work out for your good?"

I wanted to dismiss her, but I couldn't help thinking of Izzy, Amelia, and Shay. *Who would I eat lunch with if I hadn't been stuck in Drama I? Who would send me silly videos from homecoming, or make me cupcakes to cheer me up, or send texts asking how my meet was going?*

"I don't know." My words were slow and honest. "Right now, Drama still feels too hard to try and see God in it. Do you know what I mean?"

Mom's laugh had a harsh edge. "Oh, honey. I know *exactly* what you mean."

Her phone buzzed on her lap, and she tilted the screen to see it without her reading glasses. "Jennifer Cabrera."

I frowned at the van in front of me. "Why would Mackenzie's mom be calling you?"

"I have no idea." Mom put on a smile and said, "Hi, Jennifer." There was a brief silence and then, "Oh, that's because she's driving right now. We're in the car together, actually, if you want me to pass on a message . . . Oh, okay . . ." Mom gasped. "What?"

"What happened?" I asked, taking my eyes off the road. Mom gestured frantically for me to focus on driving.

"Oh, Jennifer." Mom's hand pressed over her heart. "I just can't believe it."

"Is Mackenzie okay?" My knuckles turned white on the steering wheel as I imagined all the pieces of news that could be attached to Mom's serious tone. *Car accident? Pregnant? It had been weeks since I'd heard from Mackenzie. Anything could've happened.* "What's going on?"

Mom held up a finger, the universal sign for one minute. The next exit was still a half mile away, but I put on my blinker and accelerated.

"Okay," Mom said. "Okay . . . Okay . . . I'm relieved to hear that, Jennifer. I know it can't be easy, but I think that's the best place for her right now. I'm sure you have a lot of decisions you're trying to make, but if it would help to have Tessa come down there for a visit, we can arrange that."

I pulled onto the exit ramp and parked on the shoulder.

"Okay," Mom said. "Please keep us updated and let us know what we can do. We'll be praying for you and Mackenzie both."

After a few more seconds, she said bye and hung up.

I stared at her, my mind curiously blank as I waited for the ax to drop. "What is it?"

Mom reached over and turned off the ignition, and then put her hand on my knee. "Honey, Mackenzie attempted suicide last night."

—∞—

Suicide.

The word kept blinking in my brain. All through my ride home in the passenger seat. Through the routine of emptying my swim bag and starting the laundry. Through dinner and hours of Netflix with Mom.

Suicide. Suicide. Suicide.

With the white noise of TV in the background, I scrolled my camera roll, searching for Mackenzie's face. *Did the shine of her eyes look sad beneath that smile, or was I looking too hard? Had I missed something?*

I scrolled through her Instagram. Idyllic beach shots. Pictures of her cousin and other girls I didn't recognize, everyone smiling. The filter made the photos feel light and gauzy. My stomach ached. *If someone was about to attempt suicide, shouldn't it be more obvious?*

I tried to replay our last phone call in my head. Mackenzie definitely sounded down, but I had chalked it up to being one of her bad days. She'd always been prone to high highs and low lows . . . but the lows were usually short-lived. *Weren't they? Or was she just able to bury them?*

"Maybe you'd feel better if you wrote her an email or something."

I startled to find the TV screen counting down to the next episode and Mom watching me from the other side of the couch.

"That's a good idea," I said. "I wonder if it's okay for me to call her?"

"Jennifer didn't say. Better to try and not reach her than not to try, I guess."

"Yeah."

A long silence stretched as I mindlessly scrolled Mackenzie's Instagram. I looked up and saw Mom had turned off the TV. I glanced at her. She kept smoothing the fabric of her yoga pants over her knee, over and over.

"Mom?"

She fixed me with a serious look. "Have you ever considered suicide, Tessa?"

"No, never."

"I want you to be completely honest with me."

"I am. I've never considered it."

Mom pushed a hand into her short hair and held it back from her face. "You've had a lot thrown at you this semester, and I kept thinking that you were handling everything so well. But after talking to Jennifer, now I'm wondering if maybe you're just masking the pain, like Mackenzie."

"Mom." I reached for her and she grasped my hand. "I'm not suicidal."

She held my gaze, and tears gathered in her eyes. "It's okay if you're not okay."

"I know." I squeezed her hand. "But I really am okay. Just worried about Mackenzie. I'm going to go try and call her."

"Okay." Mom squeezed back. "I'm here if you need me."

I carried my phone up to my bedroom, something I'd done hundreds of times. Never had it felt so heavy in my hand. I took several deep breaths.

"Okay, God," I murmured as I pulled up Mackenzie's number. "Please give me words. Help me swim for Mackenzie."

Her phone went to voicemail without ringing, and the sound of her cheerful "This is Mackenzie's cell phone! Leave me a message!" sent tears cascading down my cheeks. When the beep came, I wasn't sure I could even talk.

I swallowed. "Hey." The syllable warbled, and I swallowed

again. "Hey, it's me. I just . . ." I chuckled. "I maybe should have thought out what I was going to say. Um, your mom called, and I wanted to talk to you. Wanted to let you know how much I love you. How deeply I wish I could come be with you right now. I just . . ." Tears gushed from the corners of my eyes. "I'm so sorry that I didn't realize . . . If you want to talk, I'm here. Call anytime, okay? I love you, Kenz."

I hung up and wept for maybe ten minutes before I sat up and dried my eyes. I saw the gouge in my door, the one I'd made when I threw my clay cup at Dad standing on the other side, and I knew what else I wanted to say. I called back.

"Hey, me again. Remember at the party when I told everyone about my clay cup that you put back together for me after it broke?" I held back the flood of tears that pressed against my eyes. "I want you to know that the cup was even more special to me because of everything you'd done to fix it. Remember how you said you prayed the whole time you were gluing it back together that I would forgive you? *That's* why the cup is so meaningful to me all these years later, Mackenzie. And I know this is a dark time, and maybe you're feeling broken, but I also know Jesus is good at mending broken things."

Chapter
20

MONDAY MORNING, Alex came into first period with Lauren. I'd been hyperaware every time the door opened, anticipating his arrival. I had walked to Alex's house last night, wanting to tell him in person about Mackenzie, but he'd been out.

"Hi," I greeted them as they took their usual seats. They weren't holding hands or anything. That was nice. I'd mostly gotten used to seeing Alex be affectionate with Leilani, so I would adjust again. Still, nice not to have to do it right away.

Alex's smile seemed strained. "How was your swim meet?" he asked as I simultaneously asked, "How was homecoming?"

We laughed and Alex gestured to me as he slid into his seat. "You first."

"There's not much to share. I swam ten events and mostly felt good about them."

I shrugged as if that was the entire story of my weekend. *Was I even smiling? I couldn't tell.* "How about homecoming?" I asked. "Did you guys have fun?"

Alex and Lauren looked at each other.

"Yeah," Lauren said brightly. "It was pretty much what you would expect. Loud music, dancing. That kind of thing."

Alex's knee bounced beneath his desk.

"You guys looked great." My volume had unintentionally risen, reminding me of Amelia. I mentally turned it back down before adding, "I saw pictures on Instagram. You two clean up nice."

Clean up nice? Did I actually just say that?

"It was really fun," Lauren said. "Sorry you weren't able to come."

"Yeah, me too." I pulled out my MacBook and opened the lid. "There's always next year, right?"

Lauren and Alex pulled out their own computers as Mr. Huntley moved toward the front of the classroom. I took out my phone and typed a quick I need to talk to you about something in private. Could we talk after school before XC?

Even though my eyes were on my laptop, I felt very aware of Alex in my periphery. His leg continued to bounce. He checked his phone, and a second later mine buzzed with a quick reply. Sure.

———⚬———

With the One Acts being performed on Saturday, Ms. Larkin announced that all class time this week was devoted to each group having time to rehearse on the multipurpose room stage. Amelia volunteered that we go first—"Since I'm the TA and all"—and I fumbled my way through our first performance in front of actual people. My thoughts kept flitting to Mackenzie, and I filled my lines with ums and stutters, even though it was just classmates. Our twenty minutes seemed to stretch on for the entire hour, and I wanted to do cartwheels when Amelia said the last line and we could get off the stage.

"Tessa and Shay?" Ms. Larkin called as we worked as a group to carry our sets down the stairs. "Can you come here, please?"

Shay and I looked at each other, and her expression mirrored how I felt. My insides writhed with the anticipation of criticism. Izzy and I set down the cardboard bookshelf we'd been carrying, and she gave me a thumbs-up and an encouraging smile. Amelia wore an expression of relief. *Maybe that someone besides her was about to critique Shay's and my performance?*

Ms. Larkin leaned against the wall of the multipurpose room, and her gaze bounced between the two of us. "How did you feel about that, girls?"

I couldn't help blurting, "I'm really trying. I'm just not good at this."

"Me neither," Shay said.

Ms. Larkin inhaled and exhaled slowly. "Tell me more about that."

What did she mean? My thoughts had been too tangled up with Mackenzie's suicide attempt to sleep well, so maybe the meaning was obvious and I was too sleep-deprived. Only, Shay looked as confused as I felt.

"I don't know that there's much more to say." I tried to keep my voice calm and even. *Why did I feel like I was about to cry?* "I've memorized my lines and blocking, but I can't seem to be what I'm supposed to be onstage."

"Same," Shay said. "And I don't like pretending to be angry."

"Ah." Ms. Larkin considered this a moment. "Tell me, Shay, about your character's anger."

Shay shifted and kept her gaze on the ground. "Well, their older brother was killed by Nazis. Lena was closest to him, and she's very angry still."

"'Angry' is a broad category, isn't it? Everybody has been some form of angry in their lifetime." Ms. Larkin gestured to me. "Or happy, like your character, Tessa. Because those words are so vague, it can be hard to find the nuance in them and make it pop onstage. Shay, let's think about what kind of angry Lena is."

"Okay . . ." Shay pulled her hands into the sleeves of her flannel shirt. "Well, she really hates what they did to her brother. And she misses him a lot . . ."

Shay peeked at Ms. Larkin, as if trying to assess how close she was to the right answer.

Ms. Larkin nodded and asked, "Have you ever had the experience of somebody you love being hurt, and it made you angry? I don't know about you, but sometimes having a wrong committed against someone I love and care about feels way worse than if it had happened directly to me." Ms. Larkin peered at Shay. "Can you think of any similar situations in your life?"

Shay kept her gaze on the ground. She scuffed the sole of her boot on the floor. "Yeah. I guess I've felt something like that."

"Okay, great." Ms. Larkin's tone was gentle. "Then try to think of that experience as you rehearse your lines, okay? I know it may be unpleasant, and you don't have to go totally dark with it. But let's see what happens, okay?"

I was hoping that Ms. Larkin would feel that was enough instruction for both of us, but she turned her gentle smile on me. "Lucky for you, Tessa, happiness isn't quite as painful to meditate on. There's not a doubt in my mind that you've worked hard at memorization and doing things exactly as your group discussed. What I want you to do now is try to *feel*. Your character is very lighthearted, despite all the tragedy around her. Why do you think that is?"

"I don't know." My laugh had an edge to it. "Because she's naïve?"

Ms. Larkin's eyebrows rose. "Interesting. You feel her optimism is a weakness."

My underarms already felt sticky from being under the stage lights, and this conversation wasn't improving things. *Why should I have to care about dumb stuff like a fake character's feelings when I had real problems?* "Well, yeah. Considering everything going on around her, it seems like she should actually focus on fixing things or helping. Not just pretending things are fine."

"Okay," Ms. Larkin said in a way that made me think she was mentally chewing on something. "Okay, I want to come back to that. First, let's do a little emotional mining. I've done that exercise with this class, right?"

I nodded.

"Okay, so what's a time in your life that you've felt deeply happy?"

My mind went blank. I opened my mouth, hoping some light and airy memory would come floating out, but nothing happened.

Ms. Larkin watched expectantly. When a few seconds ticked by, she prompted. "When we did the exercise in class, what did you pick?"

"I don't remember," I mumbled to my shoes.

"Okay, that's fine. The memory doesn't need to be something profound or huge for it to work. Maybe a happy family vacation? Or a perfect birthday? A fun time with a good friend?"

Memories ticked by for me to choose from.

The Christmas when I was seven and my parents built the suspense all morning before gifting me the American Girl doll I'd spent months pining for. I could still picture my dad's stern face as he spoke to me very seriously about only using the wig brush with the doll's hair, and I'd giggled that my dad was so invested in the care of my doll.

Or my eleventh birthday when Alex showed up at my door with a gift—flower-shaped bobby pins that I still had tucked away in my jewelry box—even though I hadn't invited him to my all-girls birthday party.

Or Mackenzie. Ringing my doorbell that crisp spring night presenting me with my glued-together clay cup as though it were a trophy.

Ms. Larkin laid a hand on my arm. "Tessa, honey?"

With horror, I realized my jaw trembled and my eyes had filled with tears. I clamped my teeth together and looked at the wall, fighting hard to hold in the swell of emotion.

Ms. Larkin said to Shay, "Could you give us a moment?" She turned back to me and lowered her voice. "Tessa, is something going on?"

I shook my head and bit down. I could control this. I wasn't going to cry. I was fine.

"If you don't want to tell me, that's completely okay. But it concerns me when I'm trying to talk to you about happiness and you look like you're going to cry."

"I'm . . ." I cut myself off before a sob released. I swallowed. "I'm . . ." Again, I couldn't get it out. *Okay. Just say okay.*

"Tessa." Ms. Larkin's voice dipped low with concern.

I made the mistake of looking at Ms. Larkin.

Her pretty face was crumpled with concern, and her brown eyes shone with deep compassion. *How could she watch me be absolutely terrible up on the stage, and then witness me like this—messy and broken—yet still look at me with such care?*

I was horrible at her class, yet she was responding not with judgment and condemnation, but with tender kindness.

"Could I be excused to go to the bathroom?" I whispered, not able to look her in the eyes anymore, but instead staring at the turquoise rock on her necklace.

"Of course," Ms. Larkin said. "Would you like a friend to go with you?"

"No, I'm okay."

If I only could have said that a few seconds ago, the whole humiliating scene never would've played out. I pushed out the door and headed down the hallway. After several deep breaths, the wave of emotion that had risen up began to subside.

In the bathroom, I wiped my face with a paper towel and

cleaned up the eyeliner that had flaked under my eyes. After straightening my ponytail, I walked back out. Right as Alex turned the corner.

"Oh, hey." His smile hung lopsided, as if it was unsure of itself. "How are you?"

I laughed humorlessly and said, "It's a weird day."

"Yeah, I get that." He shoved his hands in his pockets. "Do you have time to talk now, or do you need to get back to class?"

"I can talk. Do you have something you need to talk about?"

Alex gave me a wary look. "Didn't *you* have something you wanted to talk about?"

I pressed my hand to my forehead. "Yes, I did. I don't know what's wrong with me today." I offered a self-deprecating laugh. "Actually, I definitely know what's wrong with me, but it's not a great topic for a five-minute conversation in a hallway. Let's wait until after school."

Alex pulled his lower lip between his teeth. "If it's about that guy on your swim team, I'd rather just get it over with instead of waiting all day."

I blinked rapid-fire. "You mean Abraham?"

"Yeah."

"No, it has nothing to do with him. Why would it have anything to do with him?"

Alex shrugged and looked at his shoes. "I thought you probably want to tell me in person," he said. "I mean, I saw already, but you wouldn't know that necessarily because I didn't like it or comment or whatever, so you'd want to tell me in person, and . . ." Alex huffed a laugh. "Now I'm rambling. Sorry."

I stared at him. His shifting feet. His crossed arms. "I don't—"

Alex looked up and stepped closer. "The thing is, I know I was a jerk last year. I know you liked me, and I was so focused on Leilani that I couldn't see what was so obvious to everyone else. And I know I probably already blew my chance with you, and that it's really not cool for me to do this when you have a boyfriend, but—" Alex swallowed—"I really like you."

"Oh," I said on an exhale.

"I've wanted to tell you all semester, but . . ." Alex smoothed his hair several times. "Everything felt complicated."

My mind was too fuzzy to grab hold of a coherent thought. "What about Lauren?"

"She was just my homecoming date, Tessa." Alex studied my face, and I wondered what he saw there. "I should've just told her no, but . . . I don't know."

He looked at me. I tried to think of a sensible response, but instead my thoughts were full of Mackenzie. While he'd been dancing at homecoming, while I'd been eating ice cream out of a carton in an Indianapolis hotel room, Mackenzie had tried to end her life. She could have been gone from this life forever.

Amelia's voice carried down the hall, along with a smattering of footsteps. " . . . should've just switched the parts. Maybe we should even do it now?"

"Don't say that," Shay answered with a groan. "I can't memorize all those new lines by Saturday."

Then Izzy, "Tessa will be fine, she just—"

The three of them came around the corner and stopped at the sight of Alex and me.

"Oh, stars! Sorry, guys!" Izzy said. "Ms. Larkin sent us to check on you."

"Yeah, I'm coming. I just ran into Alex and—"

"I'll catch up with you later," Alex said with a small wave.

"Okay," I said to his back as he hurried away.

He liked me. Alex said he liked me.

Amelia giggled, probably loud enough that Alex could hear even as he ducked into the bathroom. "What was *that* about?"

"He's in the bathroom," Shay said in a quiet voice. "Don't make her talk about it now. He could come out at any moment."

Thank you, Shay. "Yeah, let's head back."

Alex liked me. I thought if he ever said that to me, I'd be doing cartwheels down the hallway. Instead, I couldn't even get the thought to soak in, like my turtle shell was blocking even happy things now. I was trapped in here with only my sorrow and dismay for company.

"What happened in class?" Izzy looped her arm through mine as we walked. "Ms. Larkin said you asked to go to the bathroom and seemed upset."

Should I tell them about Mackenzie? They didn't even know her.

"Tessa." Amelia hung an arm around my shoulder as we walked, like a mother consoling a child. "I know what it's like not to have the performance you want. This was your first time really performing in front of other people. It will get better, I promise."

"And if it doesn't, no one will notice," Shay added with a teasing smile. "Not with how terrible I'm going to be."

"I think you'll be okay," I said, maybe stretching the truth a bit. "At least you weren't stumbling all over your lines."

Izzy still regarded me with a doubtful expression. "So, you're upset about the play . . . and that's it?"

If it was just the two of us, I would share about Mackenzie and my dad bringing Rebecca to my meet. But it wasn't just the two of us.

"Yeah." I forced a smile. "I just really dislike being bad at something, and I'm a terrible actor."

Amelia cringed. "Let's not say you're a *terrible* actor, okay? Let's say you're . . . a *growing* actor."

"We don't need to say I'm a growing actor. We can say I'm terrible."

"That kind of negative talk is bad for your psyche, though." Amelia held open the door to the multipurpose room, which was a cacophony of noise as the set was taken down from the last show.

"How about *budding*? You're a budding actor, and one day you'll be a flower."

Shay giggled. "A caterpillar actor who will someday be a butterfly."

Izzy laughed so hard she could barely get out her metaphor. "An inactive yeast actor that will someday rise and turn into a doughnut with sprinkles."

Amelia was the only one of us not amused. "Girls, I'm serious. Every negative thing Tessa and Shay say about themselves as actors translates to their confidence onstage, and . . . oh, forget it."

She marched away as we continued laughing.

Ms. Larkin crossed the room to the three of us, the hem of her khaki skirt swishing around her knees. She smiled at us before her gaze settled on me. She asked, "Doing okay, Tessa?"

"Much better, thank you."

"Izzy and Shay, why don't you go collect your things? Just about time for the bell to ring," Ms. Larkin said.

As they walked away, I told her, "I'll work on what you said. Finding a happy memory."

"Great." Ms. Larkin hugged her iPad to her chest and leaned against the wall. "There's one more thing I want you to think about. You commented that Maja is naïve. That you feel she should be making different choices."

I nodded and said, "I know I should just be able to set that aside, though. I'll work on it."

"While you're doing that, I'd like for you to consider how Maja's optimism might actually be a strength. Maybe she *is* covering up her own fear or sticking her head in the sand. Or maybe she's committed to not being defined by her circumstances. Maybe she feels she has to be optimistic because her sisters are so negative. You can decide the reason for yourself, but I encourage you to consider that Maja is not choosing to deny reality, but that she is making a choice to be optimistic in the face of suffering—and how she might actually be the strongest character in the play because of it. Can you do that for me?"

"I will do my best, Ms. Larkin."

She smiled warmly before saying, "I have no doubt you will, Tessa."

When I went to where I'd left my backpack, only Izzy and Shay were there.

"I think we maybe hurt Amelia's feelings," Izzy greeted me. "She left for lunch without us."

"I feel terrible," Shay confessed. "I'm the one who started it with that caterpillar thing."

"You didn't start it." I hooked my backpack over my shoulder. "She'll be fine in about two seconds, I bet."

As we grabbed our phones from the shoe organizer, Izzy laughed and pulled out Amelia's too. "Guess who left her phone?"

"Surprise, surprise," Shay said blankly.

We headed for the chaos of the cafeteria, and my stomach tangled up thinking of seeing Alex. He said he liked me. That he'd liked me for a while. I wanted to bask in the news and feel the delight that I should have . . . and yet, it also felt like it didn't even matter. Not in light of everything with Mackenzie. But how could I just blow off what he said when I'd been in that same place? *Hey, nice to know you like me, but I really need to talk to you about something important . . .*

When we got through the lunch line and to the table, Amelia was hunched over her tray, stabbing at her fruit salad like she wanted to hurt it.

Shay slid Amelia's slate-blue phone to her. "Hey, sorry if we hurt your feelings earlier. We didn't mean to."

"Oh, thanks. I hadn't even realized that I left my phone." Amelia thumbed open the screen and then put it back to sleep. "I know you didn't, I'm just frustrated. It feels like every time I try to encourage you two, it turns into a joke."

"We're really sorry." Shay glanced at me.

"Yeah," I added on. "We are. You're very patient with us, Amelia. I don't want to let you down."

Amelia gave us a wan smile and poked at a chunk of watermelon. "I probably have unfair expectations if I'm being honest. If my Drama II friends come to the One Acts, I want ours to be the best. I think some of them think I'm just repeating Drama I, not that I'm doing much TA stuff."

I glanced at Izzy and Shay and saw their faces looked as concerned as I felt. I hadn't realized how much pressure Amelia was putting on herself.

"Maybe we should pick a couple of days after school that we could practice?" I suggested. "Shay and I both got assignments about our characters from Ms. Larkin, and I bet under your direction, Amelia, we could really improve."

"Yeah, great idea," Izzy said as Shay said, "Sounds good."

"We don't have to do that," Amelia said into her fruit salad. "I don't want to force you guys."

"I don't feel forced. It's like studying a lot right before a test, you know?"

Amelia shrugged and said, "If that's what you guys want."

I bit my lip as I looked at her. I missed her usual energy. All her loudness and bigness that used to intimidate me were now things I enjoyed about her.

"How was homecoming?" Shay asked, clearly trying to steer us in a more cheerful direction.

My gaze unintentionally drifted to Alex—sitting at his usual table with Michael, Cody, Lauren, and friends—and then back to my friends. Izzy observed me with raised eyebrows.

"I thought it was really fun." Amelia perked up a notch. "There was a whole group of us without dates that hung out together. Didn't you think it was fun, Izzy?"

Izzy shifted her attention away from me. "Yes. Except for

having to ride with Claire and her robotics friends. That was a little weird."

"Did either of you dance with anyone?" Shay asked, then crunched into her apple.

"Mostly we danced in a group, but not during slow songs, obviously." Amelia poked a straw into her Dr Pepper. "I danced a couple of times with Wilson, this guy I know who works tech in the spring musicals. Izzy, you danced with someone, right? What was his name?"

"Miguel," Izzy said, and it took me a moment to realize she meant Michael. She shrugged and continued, "He's a nice guy, but no chemistry. Everyone thinks we should date just because we're both Mexican." She rolled her eyes.

"That's stupid," Shay said.

My gaze drifted to Alex's table again. To my surprise, I found Alex looking back at me. I blinked a few times, and then offered a quick smile and turned my attention back to my lunch.

"You know," Izzy said, bumping me with her elbow. "Maybe he would've asked you to the dance if you actually acted like you like him."

I looked into Izzy's pointed stare. Even with her hair hanging lopsided—matted down on one side and bushy on the other, as if she hadn't done much with it after getting out of bed—her stare felt intimidating.

"I mean, you posted pictures of you with that cute Abraham guy this weekend," Izzy went on. "What's Alex supposed to think?"

I wanted to throw up, that knot of guilt had pulled so tight. She was absolutely right.

"I'm lost," Amelia said. "What are we talking about?"

"Tessa and Alex."

"Ooh." Amelia's tone was chipper, as if expecting a happy tale. "What about Tessa and Alex?"

I let my hair swing on either side of my face. "I don't want to talk about it."

"Alex likes Tessa," Izzy said to Shay and Amelia as if I wasn't present. "But he won't do anything about it because, at best, she acts completely indifferent around him."

"What?" Irritation needled me. "I do *not* act indifferent."

"Oh, yes, you do. Except for when you post pictures on Instagram of you flirting with Abraham. Then you act like you prefer somebody else."

"Tessa posted pictures with a cute boy?" Amelia scrolled through Instagram on her phone. "How did I miss this?"

I liked seeing Amelia become animated again. I didn't love that it was about this topic.

"Tessa, I'm only saying this because I care about your happiness." Izzy pointed her corn dog at me, and a chunk of batter fell off with a plop into her ketchup. In another conversation, I would've laughed. "He likes you. You like him. You would be adorable together. And I love you so much that I even used the full words because I know you hate it when I say *adorbs*."

"Oh, this guy *is* cute." Amelia held her phone toward Shay, so she, too, could see the picture of Abraham and me. "Look at this, Shay."

Shay waved away the phone. "I feel creepy ogling other humans. Now, puppies or horses I'll ogle all day long."

I pushed down the shame that rose up in me at the glimpse of Abraham on Amelia's phone. "Alex . . . actually told me that he liked me."

Izzy gasped. "Oh. My. Stars. Why didn't you tell us this?"

I gathered lettuce on my fork so I wouldn't have to look at them. "Because it happened, like, twenty minutes ago. When you ran into us in the hallway."

"I knew something was going on!" Amelia declared way too loudly. "The air was electric."

"Shh," I hissed.

Amelia clapped both hands over her mouth and giggled. "Sorry."

I had no appetite but still crammed a bite of salad in my mouth, chewed, and began to gather another.

"Why aren't you Snoopy dancing on the lunch table?" Izzy asked. "You're crazy about him. This should be so exciting."

I swallowed my bite. "Yeah, I don't know. I'm just . . ." I shook my head . . . *Just sick about Mackenzie? Trying to juggle two opposite emotions at the same moment?* One thought rose from the confusion. "I don't want to get too excited. What if it doesn't work out?"

Shay frowned. "Haven't you been good friends for a long time? Why wouldn't it work out?"

"Because we're in high school." I stabbed at a stubborn carrot coin. "Because sometimes men seem worthless. There are tons of reasons why it wouldn't work out, and then I would be throwing away a great friendship."

Izzy gasped and held up both her hands in a *stop everything* kind of gesture. "I know what the problem is." She turned to me. "You're afraid it won't be perfect."

I looked away. My face felt like she'd lit a match and thrown it at me.

"I'm right, aren't I?" Izzy sounded giddy. "You go to church together, go to school together, live just a few houses away from each other. I think your moms are friends, right? And he's the only boy you've ever really liked. So what if it's not perfect? What if it's not everything you thought it would be?"

My lungs felt as though they'd physically shrunk in the last thirty seconds. *How could Izzy identify that so easily when I hadn't realized it myself?* But yes, she was right. *That* was my fear. *What if, after all these years of imagining what it would be like to date Alex, the reality didn't live up to my dream? What if it wasn't perfect?*

"Guys, I don't think Tessa wants to talk about this," Shay said softly.

"You know I'm right," Izzy pushed.

I allowed myself to nod. "Yeah, that was more true than I would like it to be."

I couldn't look at any of them. I felt like I was sitting there naked, as if my turtle shell had cracked and exposed me.

"Don't you think it would be worth it to try, though?" Amelia's voice had a tenderness reminiscent of Ms. Larkin's. "Yeah, it wouldn't be perfect because nothing is, but it could still be great."

"Maybe for a little while," I said. "But then we would break up, because that's what happens. No one marries their first boyfriend."

"That's not true," Shay said. "My grandparents never dated anybody but each other. They've been happily married for forty-something years." Her face scrunched in thought. "I guess they're happy, anyway. They're grandparents. It can be hard to tell."

"But is that all there is?" Amelia asked. "Perfection or nothing? That doesn't sound right. Even if you started dating and realized Alex isn't *the guy*, you might still experience something valuable."

I frowned. Never in my imaginings had I considered that *I* might break up with *Alex*. That was yucky to think about too.

"But—" Izzy had been leaning back in her chair and brought the front legs back onto the ground—"to Tessa it wouldn't matter really who broke up with who. That's not what she's actually worried about."

"Right," Amelia said. "Because even if she breaks up with him, it would still mean that it's not perfect."

"I'm right here, you know."

Amelia folded her hands together and leaned forward. "I'm no relationship expert, but even if it could never be perfect with Alex, it would at least be real. I would take real over the mirage of perfection any day." Her eyes latched to my face, searching. "Wouldn't you?"

I wanted to say yes, but was that the honest answer?

Chapter

21

AFTER SCHOOL, Alex was at my locker when I arrived. He'd already changed into a synthetic tee and running shorts.

I had texted Mom and asked her to pick me up an hour late. After I talked to Alex, I'd be headed to the multipurpose room to rehearse with the girls. I couldn't imagine trying to be cheerful Maja after telling Alex that Mackenzie had attempted suicide, but I didn't have much of a choice. After-school rehearsals had been *my* idea after all.

"Hey." I fiddled with my hair so it would come out from behind my ears and shield me. "Let me just switch out my books, and then we'll find a quiet place to talk."

"Yeah, sounds good." I wasn't sure if Alex was actually looking at me, because I couldn't seem to make eye contact with him. I sensed him shifting restlessly. "There's that slope heading down toward the football field. We could talk there. It's on my way to cross-country and nobody really lingers there."

"Good idea." My hands shook as I switched out my books, and I hoped he didn't notice. I wasn't 100 percent sure I'd grabbed all the correct stuff, but I could think it through after rehearsal and come back to my locker afterward.

Shay's locker was pretty close to mine, so we paused there. "Shay, I might be a few minutes late, okay?"

"Okay." She glanced at Alex and looked away. "Just don't abandon me."

"Never. Have you met my friend Alex? Alex, this is Shay. We're suffering through Drama I together."

He nodded and said, "Nice to meet you."

Shay smiled and nodded back. "Same."

"See you in a few," I said as Alex and I pushed on through the wall of students trying to get out of Northside for the day.

The sun was bright, making me wish I had sunglasses with me, and it was unseasonably warm for September 30. The humidity wasn't as intense, but it didn't really matter since I was sweating anyway. I hoped tomorrow would be cooler for my birthday.

"How's this?" Alex asked as the ground sloped toward the field. There were students around, but no one was close enough to hear us if we talked at a normal volume. It was the closest thing to privacy that you could get at school.

"Yeah, this'll work."

"So." Alex rounded to face me. "Before you say anything, I just want to apologize for what I said in the hall. It was all true, it just wasn't the way I should've told you. I'm sorry."

"You don't have anything to apologize for."

"I do." Alex shook his head, as if scolding himself. His hair flopped forward. "That was really unfair of me, especially since you're with Abraham—"

"I'm not with Abraham, actually. That was just—" this time, I shook my head at myself—"stupid swimming social media stuff. We can talk about that all later, but I had something else I wanted to tell you about. Something really awful."

Alex frowned and pushed his hair back. "What's wrong?"

"Mackenzie's mom called yesterday to tell me Mackenzie attempted suicide." Just saying the words dredged up all the confusion and emotion I'd felt last night. My eyes stung from tears.

"No," Alex said on an exhale.

My throat tightened, and I swallowed my rising emotion. "I came over to tell you last night, but you weren't there. And I thought about calling, but I hated the idea of telling you over the phone."

"I just can't believe it." Alex looked out beyond me, like answers lay over there. "Did she say why?"

"No. I left Mackenzie a couple of messages but haven't heard back yet. My mom is actually the one who spoke to Jennifer because I was driving. Sounds like they checked Mackenzie into a hospital of some kind over the weekend. Like a place for mental illness. She attempted an overdose of pills. That's really all I know."

He pushed his hair back, still looking deep in thought. "I thought she was doing pretty well in Florida. I mean, every post of hers I see on social media looks like she's living the dream life."

"I know." I wiped at the tears that slipped out. "I can't believe I was fooled by that. I can't believe I didn't realize . . ."

Alex's hand rested on my arm. "Tessa, you can't blame yourself."

More tears found their way out. "I should've been reaching out more."

"You've had a lot going on too. She could've told you that she was struggling."

"Maybe she tried, and I just wasn't listening." My voice climbed to an octave of hysteria. "Maybe if I'd asked more questions or not been so caught up in my own drama—"

"Dealing with your parents' divorce and your dad's girlfriend being pregnant is not 'drama,' okay?" Alex seemed to hesitate, and then hugged me. "You're a good friend, Tessa."

I held myself stiff against him. I didn't deserve to be comforted.

Alex took the hint and released me. "Do you think you'll go see her?"

"I want to." I swallowed. "I'd settle for just a text message right now."

Alex looked at his running watch. "I hate that I need to go, but Coach will lay into me if I'm late."

"I get it." I dried my eyes with my sleeves. "I need to go too. We can talk later?"

"Of course. I'll call you?"

I nodded and gave him a wobbly smile before turning and heading back to the school. Inside, my eyes struggled to adjust after being out in the bright sun. I should text April and Leilani to see if we could get together. They maybe didn't know yet and really should. And I should call Mackenzie again. Maybe her mom, too, if Mackenzie didn't pick up.

Lost in thought, I made my way to the multipurpose room. From outside the door, I could hear Amelia delivering one of her favorite lines with great gusto, "I give, and give, and give, but it never seems to be enough for any of you!"

I hesitated with my hand on the handle. On the other side of this door, I needed to do my best to be happy. I needed to take Ms. Larkin's advice and see Maja's optimism as a smart decision.

"Or I could do it like this," Amelia's voice bled through the door. "I give, and give, and give, but it never seems to be enough for any of you!—Which one is better?"

"I'm okay," I muttered to myself. I took a deep, bracing breath. "I'm okay."

I mentally put on my turtle shell, painted on a smile, and walked in.

───ᨒ───

Mom was running late, but since she hadn't replied to the text I sent, I assumed she was on her way.

Amelia, Izzy, and Shay had all been picked up at least ten

minutes ago. Amelia by her mom, who was on the phone and looked annoyed other than when waving to the three of us. When Mrs. Bryan smiled at us, she looked like the happiest stay-at-home mom you'd ever seen. Izzy had been next, and Claire—tasked with picking her up—had looked even more annoyed than Amelia's mom. Shay had been picked up last. She'd been in the middle of showing me some YouTube video of a celebrity horse trainer— apparently that was a thing—when a sleek SUV pulled up. I expected the driver to be the young, cool owner of Booked Up, but instead the woman looked more like the grandmother in *Gilmore Girls*, only sterner.

Practice had gone pretty well. Ms. Larkin had hung around for the first thirty minutes, which felt uncomfortable at first. But then as she cheered every time Shay and I said lines with feeling, having her there, and even the performance itself, had felt kinda fun. I even felt oddly lighthearted after pretending to be Maja for an hour. Like her optimism somehow rubbed off on me.

I scrolled Instagram, hoping for some kind of update from Mackenzie, as unlikely as that seemed. There was nothing, of course, so I gave in to temptation and pulled up Rebecca's Insta. Ever since Zoe warned me against cyberstalking Rebecca, I'd cut back. There were several new posts since I'd last checked it, but the most recent one made me feel like I'd been kicked in the gut.

How could a black-and-white thumbnail pic make me feel so much? It wasn't just Rebecca's obvious baby bump with Dad's hand resting on it, though that was painful enough. It was the way he looked at her.

He didn't just look at her, he *beamed* at her in a way he hadn't looked at Mom in ages. Maybe forever.

He looked as though he'd never been happier. Like Rebecca completed him. Like he was head over heels for her. Like a Prince Charming who'd finally found his princess. Like every other romantic cliché for someone who is deeply in love.

And what if that was because he really was deeply in love?

The thought pierced like an arrow.

What if this wasn't some midlife crisis that Dad would come to regret? What if Dad really did love Rebecca and would always be happy that he'd chosen her over Mom and me? I'd nursed this idea that in Dad's heart of hearts, he knew breaking his marriage vows was wrong and would therefore never be truly happy in his new relationship.

But looking at him then, I saw that might not be true. Dad might end up with everything he ever wanted, might get his own personal happily ever after, and there was nothing I could do to stop it.

I almost clicked away, but my eye caught on the airplane emoji Rebecca had led off her caption with. The cold fingers of dread clutched my heart as I clicked *See more.*

My guy and I are going on a dream trip! I know, I know, it's an unorthodox time for a teacher to be traveling, but the opportunity presented itself and we just couldn't turn it down!

I put my phone to sleep.

Surely not. Surely this dream trip wasn't Iceland. Dad would never do that to me.

Would he?

Even though I was outside, surrounded by oxygen, I felt like I couldn't get a breath in.

Mom's Lexus pulled into the circle drive faster than normal. I yanked open the door and fell into the SUV, barely closing the door before my heaving sobs started.

"Oh, honey." Mom put a hand on my back. "You know he's taking Rebecca, don't you?"

Chapter
22

Izzy: Where are you? I brought birthday cupcakes, and you're not here!

Izzy's text to our group thread was full of alternating cupcake and weeping emojis.

I stared at it. I should probably answer. A good person would answer.

I put my phone down and resumed staring at my ceiling.

My phone vibrated off and on for the next few minutes. Finally, I picked it back up.

Izzy: Okay, saw Alex in the hallway and he said he stopped by your house this morning and your mom said you were taking the day off. Lucky! Wish my parents would let me do that.

Izzy: BTW, how adorbs is it that Alex came to your house this morning?

She decorated this one with a dozen of the emojis with hearts for eyes.

> Shay: Tessa, don't abandon me in Drama! (Just kidding. Hope you're having fun on your special day!)

I snorted.

> Amelia: We can still eat the cupcakes at lunch tho, right? We can just send Tessa a picture. (Just teasing, T! Happy B-Day!)

I put my phone in my hoodie pocket and ignored the voice telling me that I was being rude for not responding. Or weak for skipping school today when I wasn't sick. Or ashamed that Alex had stopped by and I hadn't even come down to see him.

Mom had come up to my room and knocked softly. "Tessa, Alex is here. He wanted to say happy birthday."

I hesitated. "Can you tell him I'm still sleeping?"

"Sure, honey." And with that, she had walked back down the stairs to feed Alex my lie.

I stared at the gouge in the back of my door. It felt like a lifetime ago that I'd created that. I wanted to just fast-forward through my birthday and the dates that I was supposed to be in Iceland and the stupid One Act. *Couldn't I just be a grown-up already?*

My phone buzzed the long vibration of an incoming phone call. Probably just my dad again, but I looked anyway.

Mackenzie.

I scrambled to answer before the call slipped into voicemail. "Hello?"

"I can't believe you picked up."

Never had Mackenzie's voice sounded so sweet to me. "Of course I picked up. How are you?"

"Aren't you at school?"

"No, I'm home today. How are you?"

"I'm . . ." Mackenzie chuckled dryly. "I'm happy to be here."

Tears leaked out the corners of my eyes. "Oh, Mackenzie, I'm so sorry I didn't realize—"

"You don't need to apologize." Mackenzie's voice rose to talk over me. "I didn't—"

"I should've realized what was going on—"

"No, you couldn't have. I was working so hard to keep anyone from seeing." Mackenzie's voice sounded teary as well. "I haven't even told you that I've been on medication since Noah dumped me. I've kept a lot from you."

She'd been on antidepressants? I squeezed my eyes closed. *God, what do I say to her? What does she need to hear?*

"I'm sorry you felt you couldn't tell me," I said. "Did I do something to cause that?"

"No, Tessa." Mackenzie exhaled a laugh. "You're always so nice to me, even when I do stupid stuff. You threw that whole party for me, even though I was kinda awful to you freshman year."

"You were fine," I said, not totally sure if it was true, but Mackenzie occasionally ignoring me seemed like no big deal in light of everything else going on.

"Your messages meant so much to me." Mackenzie sounded weepy. "Maybe this is stupid, but it was like God was speaking to me through you. Telling me it was going to be okay. That He would help me put the pieces back together, just like your cup. So thank you for leaving those messages."

I wiped away tears. *Thank You, God, for giving me the right words. For helping me to swim for Mackenzie, even from a thousand miles away.* "I was happy to. I know you can do this, Mackenzie."

"My Riverbend psychiatrist changed my dosage right before we moved to Florida and added something for my mood swings. The doc at the hospital said he thought that was probably a lot of it. That he's had other patients experience suicidal thoughts on that drug combination. I hadn't had problems before, but the changes were some kind of tipping point for me. That and not having a new counselor yet exaggerated all my other problems. Being lonely here. Seeing Leilani's gazillion Snaps about homecoming with Noah. Everything just felt worse than it was."

We talked for nearly two hours. Our conversation meandered the way it used to when we'd have sleepovers and talk late into the night. Only the words felt richer because the opportunity to talk to Mackenzie had almost been lost forever. I would never again take it for granted.

When we got off the phone, I actually got out of bed. My muscles ached as if one day of lounging had been enough for them to atrophy. I stretched and paced around. On a normal day, I would have gotten home from school an hour ago.

I caught sight of my clay mug, in pieces on my desk. I rummaged through my drawer for superglue and got to work. With every piece I glued together, I prayed for Mackenzie. For healing of her heart and mind. For good, caring, Jesus-loving friends. That I would be someone she could be honest with, even about hard things like antidepressants or suicidal thoughts.

Mom knocked on my bedroom door as I glued the last piece. "Come on in."

Mom came in. "Okay, kiddo. Not to be selfish, but it's your sixteenth birthday, and I'd like to see you for a little bit today."

I leaned back in my chair, back aching. "Sorry, I was gonna come down, but then Mackenzie called."

"She did?" Mom's eyes brightened as she sat on my bed. "How is she?"

"I think she's doing pretty well, all things considered. She's home now." I filled Mom in on the things I thought Mackenzie wouldn't mind me sharing. Mom expressed her happiness that Mackenzie was doing better, and then eyed the art project on my desk.

"Did that break?"

I snorted. "Uh, yeah." I crossed the room to my bedroom door, closed it, and pointed at the damage.

"Heavens!" Mom drew closer. "Did you *throw* it?"

"Yeah. When Dad was trying to say goodbye."

Mom ran her fingertips over the splintered wood. "I can fix this for you. I just hadn't seen it."

"It's fine."

Mom turned to me. "You've had quite the year, haven't you?"

I sighed. "Not in the good sense."

"No. I'm guessing this won't be your favorite birthday either."

I shook my head.

"I think you should shower and get dressed, and then we should go out for dinner. How does that sound?"

"Not terrible."

Mom grinned, but it didn't quite reach her eyes. "I'll take that."

The shower really did feel nice. As I scrubbed shampoo into my hair, I thought of what Mackenzie said when I told her about Rebecca's Instagram post about Iceland that I'd seen yesterday, and how I'd cried so much about it, my mom said I could just stay home from school if I wanted.

"I hate that your dad keeps breaking news to you in that way," Mackenzie said in a dark voice.

I sighed. "In his defense, I basically ignore him all the time."

"Nope, we're not defending him," Mackenzie said. "There will be none of that on this call. I can't believe he didn't even tell you. Could you imagine what he would do if you changed your mind about the trip? If you were like, 'Oh, never mind, what I want most in the world is to go to Iceland!'"

We'd laughed, but now as I thought them over, the words were like a burr in my brain. *What* would *Dad do if I changed my mind?*

Chapter
23

I STOOD AT THE DOOR of the tiny house, my heart beating like I'd run here. Dad and Rebecca lived in a cute historical neighborhood full of small houses with gables, dormer windows, and detailing. One of Mom's HGTV shows would call it a neighborhood with "character" or "charm."

At dinner, I'd asked Mom if we could go by Dad's. "I'd like to tell him how I feel."

Her face clearly said *skeptical*. "On your birthday, though?"

"Yeah, I think I'd like to just get it done with."

She exhaled, puffing out her cheeks slightly. "Okay. If he says he's available, I can take you over there. It just can't take very long."

"Why?"

She hesitated. "Because I really don't want to spend your birthday sitting on the curb outside your Dad's girlfriend's house."

Well, that was fair. Dad had said tonight was perfect because Rebecca was out all night for parent-teacher conferences. That was a relief. I wasn't above doing this in front of Rebecca, but I'd prefer not to.

Dad opened the door before I could even knock. "There's the birthday girl," he said warmly.

He was in after-work clothes. Sweatpants and a T-shirt from a 5K he had run with me years ago. It felt jarring to see him wearing at-home clothes I recognized in a home I didn't.

"Hey, Dad." I kept my arms crossed, hoping to communicate loud and clear that I was not in a hugging kind of place.

"Come on in." He held the door open and gave me as much space as the tiny entry would allow.

I tried not to be obvious as I looked around, but the whole house appeared to have been painted greige and dipped in Pinterest. Hand-lettered signs encouraged choosing joy or seizing the day. Decorative pillows promoted gathering, love, and all that was fall. Nothing in here looked like it belonged to my dad.

I perched on a red armchair with a brown "Fall is my happy place" throw pillow. "Thanks for having me over even though it's last-minute."

"Of course." Dad sat across from me on a white sofa that had surely been purchased by someone who never intended to have kids. "Anytime."

He smiled at me with a tenderness that broke my heart in two. I loved him so much. With everything that had happened these last few months, I'd forgotten just how deep my affection ran for him. I'd always been a Daddy's girl.

"Something on your mind, Tessa?"

I'd just been sitting there, misty-eyed. "Yeah, actually." I clasped my hands together, so they'd stopped shaking. "I know what I said at the coffeehouse, but I've been thinking about Iceland, and I've changed my mind. I'd like to go."

I braved eye contact.

Dad's warm smile had frozen on his face. "You would?"

"Yeah. Again, I know I was mad and said a lot of stuff, but I've given it a ton of thought, and that's what I want. To go to Iceland like we planned."

Dad reached to rub the back of his neck. The pale ring of skin around his finger no longer showed. Funny how something that had taken seventeen years to make could be undone so quickly. "Okay . . ."

"I thought you'd be excited."

Dad sighed. "I'm excited you want to go still, I'm just . . . I don't know that it's the best idea."

Anger flared in my chest, and I worked to keep it out of my voice. "Why?"

"I mean, recently I can't even get you to answer my texts or talk on the phone with me. You freaked out when we came to your swim meet. So spending six days together on such a big trip just doesn't seem like a good next step for us."

"Really." The flatness of my tone must have given me away.

Dad looked at me like a deer that's heard sounds of a predator in the woods. I let the moment stretch, despite the way my heart pounded like a timpani in my ears.

"And *that's* the reason?" I said quietly. "It's not that you've already paid the money to change the ticket to Rebecca's name, because you're taking her on the birthday trip you promised me."

Dad swallowed and looked away. "You said you didn't want to go . . ."

"That's weak, and you know it."

Dad's Adam's apple bobbed. "What do you want me to do, Tessa?"

"I want you to apologize to me." The words ripped out of me, and I stood without knowing I was going to. "I want you to tell me what you did was wrong, and that after everything you've put me through, you're certainly not going to take Rebecca to Iceland. That you're just going to cancel the trip, because if you can't go with me, you don't want to go with anybody."

Dad stood too. "It's just not that simple."

"Why?"

"Tessa, of course I'd rather go with you—"

"Then take me."

Dad's eyes blazed as he stared at me. "I don't think you actually want to go. You just want Rebecca not to go."

I put my hands on my hips. "Yeah, that's true. I want you to cancel on her. I want her to know what it looks like to be on the other side of one of your broken promises."

Dad frowned. "I can't talk to you when you're like this, Tessa. This isn't you. You've always been my rational kid."

I clenched my jaw a moment to keep the tears away. "And you were always my hero, so I guess things have changed for both of us."

I stormed toward the front door, where a wooden "And they lived happily ever after" sign hung above the doorway. When I slammed the door behind me, something inside fell and clattered to the floor, and I really hoped that's what it was.

Mom put down her phone as I got in the car. "Looks like that didn't go great."

I shook my head. My eyes burned, and I couldn't seem to unclench my jaw.

She placed a hand on top of mine as we pulled away. "Did you ask him about Iceland?"

"I pretended I didn't know and that I'd changed my mind about going."

Mom groaned. "Let me guess how that went."

My throat ached from holding in tears. "Confirmed what I already knew, I guess. Despite all the texts and pleas for me to talk to him again, when push comes to shove, he'll choose her."

Mom squeezed my hand but stayed silent for a few minutes.

"I know it doesn't feel like it right now, but your dad really loves you. He's just . . . confused."

That was very generous of her. I nodded, not trusting myself to speak without sobbing. Despite how far away Dad felt, we were home in seven minutes.

As I unhooked my seat belt, I said, "I'd like to change into pajamas and eat a whole gallon of ice cream, okay?"

Mom's smile was tinged with sadness. "Whatever you want, Tessa."

I climbed out of the SUV and opened the door from the garage. The whole house was dark as night. Which was weird because normally Mom was really good about leaving on a light.

I flipped on the kitchen light.

"Surprise!"

I screamed like I'd been stabbed as Amelia, Izzy, and Shay popped up from behind the counter. Amelia blew a noisemaker, Izzy held up a plate of cupcakes, Shay's arms were up in the air, and all three of them wore party hats.

"Happy birthday!" they cried.

I gaped at them as my heart galloped frantic in my chest. "You guys! I can't believe . . ." But I couldn't get any other words out.

They'd done this for me. Here I'd ignored them all day, been a terrible and irresponsive friend, and they'd responded by throwing me a surprise party.

Their faces became blurry, and I hid behind my hands.

"Tessa, are you okay?" Shay asked.

"No." I choked on the words as they fought to come out of me. "No, I'm not okay."

—◆—

"Wow." Izzy looked like a deflated balloon, despite the party hat and body glitter she'd put on. "Your birthday has really tanked, Tessa."

"It really has," I agreed.

"I should've doubled the frosting."

Amelia selected another cupcake. "Frosting should always be doubled."

We were out on the porch, same as where I'd held the party for Mackenzie just months ago. I had walked the girls through everything. My dad leaving. The girlfriend, who became the *pregnant* girlfriend. Mackenzie's attempted suicide. Finding out about Iceland. Even the fit I threw at Grounds and Rounds.

"Oh my gosh, that was *you*?" Amelia asked. "My friend Wilson works there, and he was telling me about that."

I buried my face in my hands. "That's mortifying. He was so nice to me, and he probably thought I was such a freak."

"No. He told me your dad seemed like a real jerk, and he wanted to give you a lifetime supply of hazelnut lattes."

"That's maybe the sweetest thing I've ever heard." I leaned back in the chair. "Does that mean he goes to our school?"

"Yeah! You'll meet him when we do the spring musical."

I made a *blech* noise in the back of my throat. "It's my birthday. Don't upset me." But I smiled to show I was joking.

"I think you're really brave to share all that with us," Shay said in a soft voice.

For a moment, she looked out at the dark woods behind my house, as if considering a heavy topic. We waited, and I was just sure that Shay was finally going to reveal something big to us.

Instead, she shrugged and said, "Being honest can be hard. I'm glad you trust us."

I sighed and looked at these girls who had wiggled their way past my turtle shell and deep into my heart. Amelia, so brave and bold and encouraging. Izzy, softhearted and sweet as the cupcakes she loved to bake. And Shay, the kind and perceptive addition to our group.

Months ago, I'd sat on this patio and celebrated Mackenzie

with friends who I'd known longer, but who I allowed to see only my shallow waters. Even though I hadn't known Amelia, Izzy, or Shay as long, I knew I could trust them with my dark, murky deep end. And I hoped they would trust me with theirs too.

"I've tried for a long time to pretend I'm perfectly fine, and I'm just not." My eyes became teary again, and I struggled to get the words out even a second time. "I'm not okay."

Izzy snuggled up beside me like a puppy. "That's okay, Tessa. You don't need to be perfectly fine. We like you best when you're real."

—m—

"This one is my favorite." Mom held her phone out to me so I could see the picture of me onstage as Maja. I had a smile on my face, but the camera caught me with my eyes half-closed.

I groaned. "I look deranged."

"You do," Mom agreed. "I love it."

I rolled my eyes and took a bite of Lucky Charms. Having a cereal date after the performance had been Mom's idea, and even though it felt weird to be eating our guilty-pleasure cereals at 10 p.m. rather than after school, it also felt nice to be doing something that we had always done just the two of us. Something where Dad's absence wasn't as noticeable.

"I'm just glad it's over." I stirred my cereal. "I wish the whole class was over, honestly."

"I'm glad you're taking it." Mom tipped a little more Cookie Crisp into her bowl. "I think it's good for your comfort zone to be stretched. And it looks like you've made some really good friends in that class."

"That part's true."

"Your friend Amelia is a hoot and a half."

I grinned. Amelia had been radiant onstage, even for a measly one-act play. "She is," I said. "She's so talented."

"Izzy was quite good up there too. She seemed to really enjoy playing the pining fiancée."

I laughed. "Yeah. I think Amelia was worried she'd go over the top with it. Izzy babysits her younger brother a lot, so she always jumps at the chance for a little excitement."

Mom pursed her lips. "And I get the sense that Shay doesn't love the spotlight."

Shay had done pretty well during scenes where she had low-emotion lines, and if you were in the audience, you probably couldn't see how badly her hands trembled. But even with a week of practicing after school, her anger scenes were muted and robotic. Almost like she was afraid to let herself act angrily.

"She doesn't," I said on a sigh. "She tries hard, though."

After the play, my heart had been warmed to see Zoe, who apparently knew Shay's aunt somehow, taking extra time to speak encouragement to Shay. Seeing that made me glad that Izzy had invited her.

"I didn't want to ask, but it sounds like Shay maybe lives with her Aunt Laura? Or maybe with her grandparents? I couldn't tell."

I nodded and said, "Amelia told us her aunt owns Booked Up, and Shay lives with her in the apartment above the store."

Mom pursed her lips in thought. "There's rarely a happy reason that a child isn't living with his or her parents."

"She'll tell us when she's ready." I raised a huge bite to my mouth. "It took me a while to tell them about Dad."

"I'm sorry there was anything to tell."

"I think I'm finally understanding something you told me a while ago," I said slowly. "About using my anger to keep Dad on the hook for what he did. How it keeps me on the hook too. I think that means if I refuse to let go of my anger and forgive him, I'm going to be stuck feeling this way for a long time. Even if he's not asking for it. Even if it feels unfair. Somehow I still have to figure out how to forgive him."

"It stinks, doesn't it?" Mom reached across the table and held my hand. "I'm still wading through my own heartbreak, my own lack of control over his choices. It's much harder than the righteous anger I clung to at first."

Mom took a bite of cereal, and for the hundredth time that day, I had the thought, *I was supposed to be in Iceland today. Instead my dad is there with his pregnant girlfriend.*

"And I guess there will be a half-sibling coming along in the spring," I said slowly.

Mom rested her spoon in her bowl. "There will be."

"I feel guilty for not being excited. New life should always be celebrated, right?"

Mom blew out a breath. "Yes, but it's okay to not be okay about the baby. I think it'd be a good idea for you to see a counselor. Help you process all those emotions."

There was a part of me that resisted the idea. Surely, I would be fine. I could figure this out on my own. But this could also be another piece of letting Jesus swim for me, inviting in professional help.

"I will try to be okay with that."

Mom turned her phone to me. "On a happier note, look what I got a picture of tonight."

I tried to groan but giggled instead. "Oh, Mom."

The picture was of Alex and me, off on the side of the multi-purpose room. I had on my Maja costume and intense stage makeup. Alex looked like Alex in his shorts, Northside Cross-Country hoodie, and floppy hair. Mom had snapped the shot as he handed the rose to me.

"What's this for?" I had asked. I'd been agitated that he was even there. The fewer people in the audience, the better. I especially didn't need Alex witnessing my debut stage performance.

"My mom said it's traditional to give flowers to actors after a performance."

I rolled my eyes, even though my stomach felt like I'd swallowed grasshoppers. "I haven't even earned it yet."

He'd grinned. "I'm giving it before because you don't have to earn it," he said. "Whatever you do up there—forget lines, trip, whatever—it's not going to change what I think of you."

"Oh, it might."

"Nope. It won't. You know that swim meet in August when you swam for that little girl?"

Wow, subject change. "Uh, yeah."

"Do you remember what you said afterward in the car?"

I shook my head.

"You said we all need someone to swim for us sometimes." Alex swallowed. "And all I've wanted these last few months is to be able to swim for you."

Tears filled my eyes and I hurried to blink them away. Amelia would yell something fierce if I cried off my stage makeup that she'd so laboriously applied. "I know you've been trying, and I've been pushing you away. I promise I won't do that anymore."

Alex squeezed my arm. "Okay."

"I gotta go."

"I know. Break a leg."

I felt myself blushing like crazy as I had carried the rose backstage to get in position. The girls had fawned over the flower—well, mostly Amelia and Izzy—and the boost in my mood had helped me hit Maja's optimistic tone the best I had done yet. I was finally understanding what Ms. Larkin had meant, that how Maja opened herself to happiness even in the hardest of times actually took great courage.

Mom stood and rinsed her bowl, and I opened my phone to scroll Instagram.

April and Leilani appeared to be doing some kind of spa night and had a whole series of pictures of them in mud masks with cucumber slices on their eyes.

Abraham had pictures of him and Lexi at swim practice this week.

Mackenzie had posted a quote about loneliness.

Love you, friend, I commented. **Looking forward to our video-chat date tomorrow!**

Lauren had taken artful photos of the new makeup she'd received in the mail, with promises for a "fall palette tutorial" in the coming days.

Alex had told Lauren about liking me, and to her credit she'd been gracious about it. She'd told me privately that they didn't have as much in common as she thought they did, and that even she felt homecoming was a bust. "At least I have good pictures, though," she'd said.

A text from Izzy came through to our group chat—**Didn't want to share this pic on social but it's my fave from the night**—and I clicked away from the picture-perfect world of Instagram to a photo of the four of us making ridiculous faces in our overdone stage makeup. I laughed out loud.

"What are you laughing about?" Mom asked.

"This picture Izzy got of us." I turned the screen to my mom, and she smiled.

"I love seeing you act silly," Mom said with a sigh. "There's been so little of that these last few years."

Amelia texted, **Why not share? This is who we really are.**

I studied the picture a little closer. Everything about Amelia's pose was big—wide eyes, jazz hands, open mouth. Izzy made a face that was pure innocence, her face tilted and resting on clasped hands, an angelic smile on her face. Shay looked as though she was trying to make an angry face; her nose was wrinkled, her eyes narrowed, but she was smiling, unable to follow through.

And I, again, had a semi-deranged look on my face. I'd been

going for "surprised" or "shocked" but somehow wound up looking as though I hadn't expected the picture to be taken yet. Maybe
I hadn't.

   Agreed, I wrote back. **I'm posting it! #realnotperfect.**